Warriors of the Andes

Other Avalon Books by Clifford Blair

GUNMAN'S ODDS
BROTHERHOOD OF WARRIORS
DEVIL'S CANYON DOUBLE CROSS

WARRIORS OF THE ANDES

CLIFFORD BLAIR

AVALON BOOKS
THOMAS BOUREGY AND COMPANY, INC.
401 LAFAYETTE STREET
NEW YORK, NEW YORK 10003

F
BLA

PRINTED IN THE UNITED STATES OF AMERICA
BY HADDON CRAFTSMEN, SCRANTON, PENNSYLVANIA

With love to my mother, who frowned on those
wild adventure novels I read as a kid. Here's
hoping you enjoy this one.

Chapter One

Doug Bonner saw the three men and read the danger in them. They lounged in front of the dingy bar. The establishment seemed to be the major point of commerce and social life in this isolated village in the Peruvian Andes.

He kept his pace steady as he neared them. He could feel their hungry eyes fixed on him. He raked them with his own gaze. What did they read into his casual Western garb, his longish hair, and obvious identity as an American? Drugs, of course. Only the international trade in such substances would bring foreigners like him to this place. Were they part of the trade too?

He was relieved that they saw him as no more than a young American dealer here to make a purchase of one or more of the illicit drugs that had their origins in this region. He was sure that they had not discerned his true identity as a deep-cover agent for the U.S. Drug Enforcement Agency.

The three men were of mixed Indian descent. He

saw in them the breed of violent men drawn to the remote and primitive areas across the world where the law held little sway. One of them carried a machete from a thong on his wrist. Another had a combat knife sheathed at his waist. The third was so big that he probably believed he didn't need weapons. Their clothing was shabby. They were at home here.

El Dolor, the town was called. Translated, it meant The Pain. The name was grimly appropriate, Doug thought, for what might prove to be the source of the insidious Devil Dust.

The trail here had been a long one. It had begun in the United States, where a deadly new substance was spreading like a contagious virus through the drug culture. Devil Dust was a suitable name for the mysterious drug known for ecstatic and addictive highs, and also a propensity for homicidal madness and a horrifying ten percent mortality rate. Unchecked, the drug would eventually infest all levels of society in the same fashion as its less-lethal forerunner, cocaine. In his tracing of the origins of the drug, Doug had, in his months spent undercover in Latin America, perceived a murky pattern of rumor and speculation that centered around El Dolor.

Grim-eyed men in decaying bars had whispered of the town. They spoke of a newly formed underground cartel that wielded vast political power. It was the only source of the pulpy vegetable base of a deadly new drug. Tales were repeated of a powerful and reclusive drug lord who was never, under any circumstances, to be crossed. He was served, it was said, by assassins of inhuman strength who could not be killed. And this drug lord might be contacted only in El Dolor.

The town was an enclave of dissolute and abandoned humanity. It crouched amidst the remote and windswept peaks of the Andes. From the main street, Doug could see the rugged vastness of the surrounding mountains in the pale afternoon sunlight. Huge regions of this range, he knew, remained unexplored by outsiders except for aerial surveys and mappings.

Doug had been in El Dolor for two days, and was awaiting the contact he had been promised by a fearful mid-level dealer in Lima, the nation's capital. He was on his own. There would be no backup if things went sour. Security had dictated deepest cover. His presence was unknown to even the Peruvian authorities. "Follow the trail as far as you can," he had been ordered by his superiors in the DEA. "And then get out." If he could, Doug had added mentally.

He looked past the bar and the trio of desperadoes. A newish four-wheel-drive vehicle of American make was parked in front of the town's general store. He had not seen it before. It was an unusually valuable vehicle for this locale. His own conveyance was an ancient battered Jeep. El Dolor could only be reached by four-wheel drive, on horseback, or by foot or helicopter. He wondered who had brought the late-model vehicle to this backwater town.

He dismissed his speculations as he neared the bar.

As the trio of desperadoes eyed him with violent avarice, he was grateful for the .45 in the waistband of his jeans at the small of his back. The gun was an IBM A-1 .45 automatic, vintage World War II. It was a nonregulation weapon for DEA agents, but had served Doug's grandfather well in the war, and his father after that in a long career as a police officer. It had served Doug equally well in the drug raids and combat situations that had been, all too frequently, a part of his years as an undercover agent.

Most of the DEA agents of Doug's age favored the new high-tech 9 mm assault weapons. But from harsh experience, Doug knew and trusted the .45. Ready for what might come, he carried it cocked and locked, with a round in the chamber. All that needed to be done was to flip off the safety and pull the trigger.

He had disassembled the .45 to smuggle it into the country. It was forbidden for DEA agents to go armed here even when on official assignment. As on past missions, he had ignored the prohibition.

The desperado with the machete at his wrist made a jerking motion with his arm. It flipped the hilt of the big knife up into his palm with practiced ease. Doug resisted the impulse to draw the .45. It would be stupid to use a prohibited firearm against rabble like these.

He locked gazes with the machete man as he mounted onto the low porch fronting the bar. His senses were alert for movement from either of the other two. After a moment the machete man let the heavy knife drop to dangle from his wrist thong. Doug shouldered past them into the bar.

He felt almost as though he had entered a cave. Or a tomb. Lanterns on rickety tables and small windows provided the only illumination. Doug flinched at the odors of alcohol and filth. The bar itself consisted of a wide board nailed to empty oil drums. Doug stepped to the side of the doorway and surveyed the room.

Some of the tables were occupied by dimly seen shapes. Near him, two men were arguing over a ragged fighting cock in a small cage. The bloody and sadistic practice of cockfighting was a popular pastime here, he knew.

He glanced toward the mountain-bellied barkeep. Wordlessly the fellow pointed. Doug saw a small figure at a table in the far corner. Skirting the cockfighters, he approached the man.

Dark, twitching eyes gazed up at him from a wasted face. Doug found it hard to watch them. Most of the man was invisible beneath a shabby poncho. A gun was probably invisible there also, Doug guessed.

"You are Ramon," he said in Spanish.

"You are the gringo." Ramon's voice was a harsh rasp.

Doug swung out a handmade chair and positioned it so that he could see Ramon as well as the rest of the barroom. Ramon had a beer in a dirty mug in front of him. A hand-rolled cigarette smoldered on the table. Doug smelled marijuana in the sluggish tendril of smoke.

"What do you want, gringo?"

"No more games," Doug whispered. "You know what I want. You've had me watched and checked. I want an answer. I've got better things to do than stay in this filthy place."

Ramon's thin lip curled in contempt. Only one of his hands was visible. Doug watched for motion beneath the poncho.

Slowly Ramon picked up the smoldering joint. His twitching eyes were fixed on Doug's face. He sucked deeply on the cigarette. The hit of grass had no apparent effect on him. He withdrew the joint from his lips.

Doug reached out casually and flicked his fingers hard against Ramon's hand. The smoldering joint spun away like a meteor. Pain and fear flared in Ramon's twitching eyes.

"I warned you." Doug's voice was quiet and hard. "You're not important enough to play games with me. I want an answer."

The simple show of force had apparently broken Ramon's shaky nerve. He was obviously a creature subservient to others. He cringed beneath his poncho. "Lord Aguilar will see you," he said hoarsely.

"When?"

"Tomorrow," Ramon stammered. "I will take you

there. It is in the mountains. We must drive for several hours and then go on foot a distance."

Doug settled back in his chair. He did not think the little man was lying. "All right," he agreed. "I'll meet you in this bar." He did not bother to set a time.

"*Sí,*" Ramon said hurriedly. "I'll be here." He seemed suddenly eager to depart.

Doug nodded a curt dismissal. Ramon scurried for the door. He had to swerve to avoid colliding with the man and woman who had just entered the bar. Doug stared at the newcomers. He now knew who had brought the late-model four-wheel drive to El Dolor.

The pair were obviously American. The woman was not much past twenty, and she had an athletic figure clad in jeans and a designer T-shirt. Her brown hair was pulled back behind her ears as if to keep it out of her way. Strength and intelligence shone from brown eyes in a face that was compelling as well as beautiful. Doug did not want to stop looking at her.

Her companion was older—thirty perhaps. His tanned features were handsome in an intellectual sort of way. He had razor-cut brown hair and wore khaki pants and a multi-pocketed shirt like an African explorer on a late-night movie. A large calculator of some sort was in a holster on his belt. His carriage was that of a yuppie athlete who favored tennis and probably racquetball.

Looking at them, Doug felt a prickling of disquiet. These two were as out of place here as Ramon would be on a college campus. And clearly, they were oblivious to the fact. *Babes in the wood,* Doug thought. *Innocents in the kill zone.* He was surprised that the trio outside had allowed them to enter.

The woman had become aware of his gaze, and she was studying him curiously. He knew that in his guise as an American drug dealer he must look in place in these surroundings. He was irrationally sorry for that fact.

Her companion was surveying the other occupants of the bar. Plainly the pair were seeking someone or something. Finally he settled his attention on the slovenly barkeep. "We need a guide," he said in classroom Spanish. "We will pay well."

The man was an idiot to boast of his wealth in a place like this, Doug thought. At the very least, he owed it to them to warn them of their danger, even if it meant breaking character.

Before he could move, figures stirred in the doorway. A tightness gripped Doug's muscles. The three desperadoes from outside had followed the newcomers into the bar.

Their intentions were obvious. Barbaric greed gleamed from their coarse features. They spread out in an arc before the door, blocking the only route of escape. The woman looked around and saw them. She shrank toward her companion. He turned.

"What do you want?" he demanded.

The machete man grinned lasciviously. "El Demonio would like this one." He leered at his companions. "But he is not here and we are." He flipped the machete into his hand.

Doug wondered what kind of man it might be who went by the name of the Demon. The big desperado reached for the woman.

Doug leaped up. "Enough!" he snapped. So much for staying in character, he thought grimly. But he could not stand mutely by and see murder done. And worse.

The machete man snarled at him like some predatory beast. "This is no concern of yours, gringo."

Doug gestured at the intended victims. "Leave them alone and you can walk out of here," he told the machete man. "Otherwise, you'll crawl out. I promise."

The machete man glanced at his companions. It was an obvious signal for them to be ready.

"Get out of the way," Doug said to the woman. Her companion appeared bemused. He looked from Doug to the menacing trio and seemed about to speak. The woman grabbed his arm and dragged him clear.

"As you say, gringo," the machete man conceded. He let the hilt of the machete fall from his hand. Instantly then, he flipped it back up in his grip. Jerking the blade overhead, he howled. The three of them came at Doug simultaneously.

Doug went to his right, toward the machete man. He wanted that one out of the way first.

The heavy blade cut down at his skull as he came

in. Adroitly Doug swiveled his torso aside. The blade cleft the air past him. He swept his left arm out to block his foe's arm from rising. Off balance from his missed stroke, the desperado lurched forward. Doug lifted his knee and snapped his foot out. The hard toe of his combat boot rammed into his foe's body beneath the ribs.

The desperado jackknifed forward. Doug shot out the heel of his palm. It met the descending face squarely between the eyes. The machete man toppled limply to one side.

Doug turned to face the rush of the thug with the combat knife. The blade was out now. Doug made no effort to block or check the man's headlong attack. Instead, he whirled back to his left, out of the path of the knife. His left leg rose as he spun in a half circle. His booted heel caught the knife man in the small of the back as the fellow hurtled past. The impact bent him backward like a drawn bow. Doug completed his spin, clenched hands lifting. He hammered the edges of his fists to the sides of his foe's vulnerable neck. The thug's face hit the floor as he fell.

Doug had an instant's awareness of the bulk of the third desperado looming hugely over him on his right. The man's massive arms were outspread. There was no place to turn, no way to escape the mauling embrace. Doug set himself as the great arms started to close about him. He caught his right fist in his left hand and used the strength of both arms to thrust his right elbow deep into the giant's swollen belly. Foul air from the brute's lungs hit him in a stifling blast. Still gripping his right fist, he jerked his elbow back, then drove it up to the unshaven chin. Pain streaked through his arm. The bulk of the huge man seemed to hang suspended over him.

He jerked his arms back into a cocked position. His right arm was folded across his chest; his left arm was straight back at an upward angle. He snapped both arms out, twisting his torso into the move. The edge of his right palm chopped like a sledgehammer against the big man's temple. The impact rocked Doug down through the soles of his boots. He was barely able to sidestep as the bulky figure fell inertly to the floor.

Doug stood over him for a moment. Then he turned toward the out-of-place couple. They were staring with wide eyes. Doug was just beginning to breathe hard as his exertions took their toll.

"Who are you?" he asked. It came out more harshly than he had intended.

The words seemed to break the spell. The woman flinched. The man drew himself up almost arrogantly. "I'm Professor Dickinson Tyler," he announced. "This is my research assistant, Ellen Rogers." She looked at Tyler admiringly as he introduced her.

"What are you doing here?" Doug's tone was still too harsh. He didn't care.

The professor took offense. He glared as if confronting a classroom of unruly students.

The young woman filled the gap in conversation: "We're here on an archaeological research grant from Oklahoma State University." Her voice was husky. She appeared intent on forestalling any pending comment from Tyler. "Thank you for helping us," she rushed on. "I've never seen anybody fight like that except in the movies. I didn't think anybody could do that for real."

Tyler snorted in what might have been contempt. "It was hardly necessary," he said loftily. "We could have come to terms with those men without violence."

"*Their* terms," Doug said coldly. "You dead and she at their mercy."

Tyler's mouth snapped open, framing what would obviously be an angry retort.

"Please, Dick." Ellen laid a restraining hand on his arm. Doug could imagine the warmth of her touch. She gazed up at Tyler imploringly. He turned stiffly away, cutting himself off from the conversation.

Ellen stepped closer to Doug. He became acutely aware of her appeal and femininity. "Don't be offended, please. Dick—Professor Tyler—is very capable. He's traveled all over the world. He's the youngest full professor the university has ever produced. This is my second trip with him to South America."

Her sincerity mollified Doug slightly. He avoided

looking at the stiff figure of the young professor. "Archaeology?" he asked.

Tyler turned back as if he had received a cue. Apparently, he had overcome his anger. "That's right," he said crisply. "Ellen and I are researching evidence of the existence of an ancient and highly developed prehistoric Indian civilization in this region."

"The Incas?" Doug asked. Before its conquest by the Spaniards, the Inca Empire had dominated much of the South American continent.

Tyler blinked as if surprised at Doug's knowledge of even this common bit of information. "No," he answered. "Not Incan, but influenced by them and similar to them in many ways, we believe. Confirmed evidence of their existence here during prehistoric times would revise present historical concepts and verify a number of my own theories."

Doug imagined him lecturing pompously in front of a classroom of bored students. "If you're smart," he said, "you'll clear out of here before you get into even more trouble. These boys were bush league compared to some of the other players around here." He gestured at the stirring desperadoes. "And that's no theory."

Tyler's dark eyes flashed. "We've neither asked for, nor do we desire, your dubious assistance or your questionable opinions," he said.

"Be thankful for both," Doug shot back.

Ellen stepped between them. "You're an American, aren't you?" she asked Doug quickly. "What's your name?"

Doug hesitated, then he told her.

"Are you here on business?" she persisted.

"Yes," he answered after a moment.

"What kind?"

"The kind where he wouldn't want the Peruvian or American authorities to ask very many questions, I'd guess," Tyler interjected shrewdly.

"Oh!" she said. For the first time, the significance of Doug's outlaw appearance and the most obvious reason for his presence here seemed to dawn on her. Drug running was big business these days. It also played an important role in the underground economies of many Latin American countries. Dealers looking to make big scores often came to the source to make their buys. Ellen shrank back toward Tyler.

Doug held his face expressionless. Whatever ground he had gained with her had just been lost, thanks to Tyler's shrewd appraisal of him. Intellectually, the man was not a fool. But to openly accuse a stranger of being a drug smuggler in these lawless environs showed a lack of both common sense and street savvy. Doug resisted the idiotic impulse to blurt out his true purpose here and regain Ellen's good graces. Both of these people seemed capable of arousing swift, strong emotions in him.

"Just remember that you've been warned," he said. "These three might not bother you again, but there'll be others like them. Or worse." The fallen attackers had recovered sufficiently to stagger from the bar. Doug added, "My advice is to go back to the university and do your studying out of books. Either that or get an armed escort from the government to accompany you."

"That won't be necessary." Tyler drew himself up. He was as tall as Doug. "And your advice is superfluous. Ellen, we can do without a guide. I've memorized and programmed the aerial survey maps of the region." With easy familiarity, he withdrew the large calculator from its sheath on his belt. He held it in the palm of one hand, the fingers of his other poised over it. His high, intellectual brow furrowed in concentration. Then his fingers danced agilely over the tiny keyboard. The device emitted a shrill series of high-pitched fluting sounds that made Doug want to scratch his ears. *Some kind of miniature computer,* he thought. Tyler was obviously a maestro with it.

Tyler nodded in confirmation of whatever data was displayed on the small digital screen. "Yes," he said, replacing the computer in its sheath with evident satisfaction, "I'm confident we can reach the site without assistance." His hand caressed the computer as though it were a fetish.

Ellen nodded. She obviously had confidence in her mentor. Her eyes touched Doug briefly, then shifted away. He guessed that she was hurt that he had not denied Tyler's blunt accusation.

"Let's be on our way, Ellen," Tyler ordered. "I've

had enough of this place." He led the way toward the door.

"Take care," Doug said.

Ellen turned to glance at him before they went out. Her expression, Doug thought, was troubled.

Chapter Two

The chill wind whipped down across the barren plateau from the surrounding peaks of the Andes. It carried a cruel bite, Doug thought, but it was no more cruel than the eyes of the man he faced.

Salvador Aguilar had brought two bodyguards with him to this remote meeting place. Doug suspected that there were more of them concealed in the rocks. In addition there was Ramon. Doug was glad of the cocked and locked .45 in the waistband of his jeans. Extra clips were in his pockets.

Simon was the more dangerous of the bodyguards. Tall and lean, he watched Doug with the intensity of a wolf eyeing an intruder in his territory. He carried a Mac-10 assault gun, which was sophisticated armament for the head bodyguard of a South American drug lord. But it was not the gun so much as Simon's feral aura that convinced Doug of the man's potential as a killer.

Simon's companion was a sallow-faced youth. Doug had not heard his name. He had a Remington pump shotgun with a sawed-off barrel. It was slung casually over a thin shoulder by a rope. The shotgun was not as sophisticated as Simon's weapon, but it could be equally effective in killing a man. The youth appeared eager to prove as much. A backpack was also slung on his narrow back.

Aguilar, their chief, appeared to be unarmed, but Doug guessed that there were some nasty surprises under his colorful poncho. Aguilar came across as soft and almost fragile. His build was slender, and his features just missed being delicate. Doug didn't trust that impression for a moment. In his own way, Aguilar was more dangerous than either of his paid killers.

"You have come a long way to meet me, señor." Aguilar's normal tone carried a consistent edge of mockery, Doug was learning.

"My people thought it important that we contact you," Doug answered politely. "You appear to be the principal source of a commodity for which we have an avid market."

Aguilar smiled. "I am the *only* source," he corrected gently.

"Then my people wish to deal with you."

"Your people have power and influence in your country," Aguilar conceded.

Doug did not let his relief show on his face. His cover story and his phony background had held up under whatever scrutiny they had been subjected to by Aguilar. "That is true," he agreed. "They would make good contacts and customers for you."

Aguilar bared his teeth. "You are young to be their representative."

"I'm old in experience."

Aguilar looked into his eyes, and then turned his gaze to the barren and stony wastes around them. "There are others who already buy what I have to sell," he said. "They pay a high price and would not be happy to have me selling to yet another buyer."

"What do you care, as long as you control the market?"

Aguilar chuckled. Like his smile, the sound had no mirth. "Exactly," he agreed. "You would make a fine businessman."

"I am a businessman," Doug answered. The words had a grim sound in his own ears. *My business is death and drugs and killers like Aguilar and Simon,* he thought bitterly. He was too young to be as old as he felt. Maybe he had been in this game too long. *How many times have I played this grim charade?* he asked himself. Too many, but never had the stakes been so high or the players so dangerous.

"And I, too, am a businessman," Aguilar said. "I will sell to you, but the price will be high. Are you prepared to pay it?"

"I will pay it," Doug told him, "but only when the product is in my hands."

"Of course, Señor Bonner, of course." Aguilar turned his gaze to the edge of the plateau and the mist-shrouded valley that lay below. Tendrils of white fog reached up like blind, subterranean creatures seeking light and air. The floor of the valley was invisible. Its depth and size were impossible to guess. On all other sides of the plateau, rugged mountains thrust barren rocky peaks skyward. Snow glinted sharp and white in the sunlight on the highest summit.

Aguilar drew his eyes back from the shrouded valley. "My suppliers will be here shortly with the merchandise."

Doug frowned. *What suppliers?* he wondered.

Beneath him the ground seemed suddenly to heave and roll. For a brief, horrific moment, the entire panorama of desolate peaks shifted before his vision. Atavistic fear pumped adrenaline through him. He caught his balance as the heaving of the earth subsided.

"Earth tremor. This region is prone to them." Aguilar's bland explanation hinted at subtle mockery. But beneath it, Doug detected fear.

He did not blame the drug dealer for being afraid. The sensation of having the earth turn to jelly beneath his feet was not one he cared to experience again. He heard a distant rumbling that diminished to trembling silence. Somewhere, he guessed, the side of a mountain had been torn away by the shaking of the earth, to plunge into an abyss never seen by the eyes of man.

He felt the predatory look of the gunman, Simon,

upon him. He returned the killer's gaze, hoping that his instinctive, gut-wrenching fear hadn't shown on his face. After a moment Simon looked away.

Aguilar had turned an expectant gaze once more on the shrouded valley. Doug looked too. His muscles bunched reflexively as he saw the figures emerging from the haze.

In single file they ascended an almost invisible path that wound through a forest of rocky outcroppings. Doug counted a dozen figures. There could have been more lurking behind in the fog.

Looking like apparitions from some bygone barbaric age, they were primitive pale-skinned warriors. They wore laced leather boots, leggings, and furred vests that bared their sinewy arms and much of their muscular chests. Their long hair, looking almost bleached, was worn in twin backward-curving clubs like the horns of a bighorn sheep.

Next, Doug noted what appeared to be carefully crafted stone daggers slung at their waists. Their heavier armament consisted of elaborately carved stone war clubs. The heads of the clubs were skillfully tooled to portray the fanged, gaping jaws of some reptilian beast. Wielded by trained hands, such weapons could be devastating in close-in fighting.

As they drew nearer, Doug saw that their pale faces had much of the broad flatness of the native Indian tribes descended from the ancient Incas. In addition, they had the deep chests necessitated by the thin air of these altitudes. But they were taller and more lithely muscular than other Indians of the region. Doug thought with a chill that they might almost be ancient statues, carved from marble and brought to life, marching up from the dim past.

He forced his attention to Aguilar and his underlings. There was no surprise in their faces; the strange warriors were not new to them. But there was a predatory wariness to their features now, as if they recognized in the newcomers a source of danger.

Were these Aguilar's mysterious suppliers? Doug wondered. Were they the elusive source of Devil Dust?

"I have never brought a buyer to meet with my suppliers," Aguilar told him softly. "I do this to accommodate you, since you insist that time is of the essence. You should feel flattered."

The man's greed for a fast sale to a new buyer had probably done more to motivate him than any sense of courtesy. "These are your suppliers?" Doug asked. "Who are they?"

"You do not need to know that." Aguilar turned away with a swirl of his colorful poncho.

Doug saw that all the pale warriors, except for the apparent leader, carried hide sacks slung over their shoulders. He felt a prickling along the nape of his neck. He had accomplished his mission. He had traced Aguilar to his suppliers. But, in a sense, he knew less now than when he had started.

As the warriors reached the summit of the plateau, the leader stepped forward while his fellows spread out in a defensive arc behind him. The leader hefted his artistically carved stone club easily in one hand and posed as if for the opening rites of some pagan ceremony. Even posed, he struck Doug as formidable.

He stood well over six feet in height, making him the tallest of his party. He had the superb musculature of a weight lifter coupled with the sinewy, functional grace of an all-around athlete. His features were handsome and arrogant at once.

The chieftain's onyx eyes flicked shrewdly over Aguilar and his companions. His gaze held longest on Doug. There was no discernible change of expression, but the subtle tensing of the man's muscular body told Doug that the warrior was not pleased with his presence.

Aguilar stepped forward. He was almost fawning before the towering warrior. "I welcome Cortozca, the honorable Queen's Warrior." He spoke in Quechua, a language descended from that of the ancient Incas and widely spoken among the Indian population. Doug had acquired a fluency in it from past missions to South America.

"Who is this one?" Cortozca demanded in strangely accented Quechua. He snapped the heavy war club straight out from his shoulder to point at Doug. Held at arm's length, the fanged head of the club did not tremble, Doug noted. As a feat of sheer strength, it was enough to impress him. "The God of the Dark Waters is angry at his presence. The God has caused the earth to move."

"He is an associate," Aguilar answered smoothly. "He is to be trusted. Your God of the Dark Waters is not angry."

The pale face darkened with emotion. "You tread near the edge of the precipice to bring interlopers here." The warrior's voice was as deep as the mighty chest from which it rumbled.

"I would not betray the Queen's Warrior." Aguilar bristled a little bit. Apparently, there were limits to which he would allow himself to be intimidated by even his awesome supplier. Doug sensed the uneasy relationship between the two men. He wondered what Aguilar was using for barter.

The warrior lowered his club. He still showed no sign of strain. Apparently he had decided to ignore Doug's presence. "I have the Fire Lichen." He used his other arm to gesture at his burdened followers. Perhaps holding the club at arm's length had been an effort after all.

Aguilar bobbed his head. "And I have many of the healing kits. A sample." He motioned forward the nameless youth with the shotgun. From his backpack the youth extracted what Doug recognized as a basic first-aid kit. He extended it to Aguilar, then stepped back. The drug lord passed it to Cortozca. The warrior examined it almost contemptuously.

So this was the coin in which Aguilar traded for the Devil Dust. Doug thought that there was something obscene about using medical kits to barter for drugs. But medical supplies would be valuable to whatever primitive tribe Cortozca represented.

"One day," Cortozca said ominously, "I will barter with you for your weapons, not these healing kits. They are for women and children." His hungry gaze sought out Simon's Mac-10.

Aguilar looked uneasy. The prospect of his supplier having access to high-tech assault weapons clearly did not set well with him. Doug wondered what prevented Cortozca from pursuing such a deal even now. Was it some political or religious precept of his tribe?

Cortozca was obviously ambitious. Doug surveyed the warriors at his back. Some of them appeared almost as formidable as their leader. The idea of their being armed with assault weapons and motivated by pagan savagery was not a pleasant one.

A woman's voice was raised in protest. A man's voice joined it. Doug turned in the direction of the sounds. He was aware of the others grouped there on the plateau doing likewise.

Five figures came into view from the surrounding rocks. Three of them were gunmen of the same stamp as Simon and the youthful shotgun bearer. The ground seemed to shift once again under Doug's feet as he recognized their captives.

Professor Dickinson Tyler and his assistant, Ellen Rogers, looked angry, disheveled, and frightened. Their captors had obviously not been gentle with them. They were dressed for fieldwork, she in jeans, he in khakis. Doug noted that the miniature computer was still in its belt sheath. In addition, each of them carried a belt-clipped walkie-talkie. Doug noted that they were the latest high-tech models.

One of the gunmen gripped Ellen roughly by the arm. Another shoved Tyler forward. Even from thirty feet away, Doug could see the gunman's eyes glowing with the yellowish fire of a user high on Devil Dust. He felt a chill of horror.

"We caught them spying!" the third gunman called out in Spanish. He had some kind of sawed-off pump shotgun.

"We weren't spying!" Ellen cried out angrily. "We're archaeologists! We were looking for—" She broke off as her wide eyes fell on Doug with startled recognition.

Aguilar looked sharply from her to Doug. "Do you know these intruders?" he demanded.

Doug tried to keep his face impassive. "I ran into them in town," he answered. His mind was churning frantically. The pair's presence here could be disastrous for him as well as for them.

"Ellen! Look!" Tyler was staring raptly at Cortozca and his party of warriors. He seemed all but oblivious to any danger. "Living remnants!" he cried. "Descendants of the lost tribe! Do you know what this means?"

Doug had all too good an idea, although it probably did not jibe with that of the professor. He looked quickly at the warriors. Cortozca's face was once again dark with rage.

"More interlopers?" the warrior chieftain snapped. "What is the meaning of this?"

Aguilar told him, "I'll take care of it." An ugly light grew in his eyes as he studied Ellen. Ignoring Tyler, he strode forward to stand in front of her. "What are you and your friend doing here?"

Tyler seemed to become aware of the threat of danger. He took two steps and thrust himself between Aguilar and Ellen. Aguilar had to retreat a pace. Tyler did not lack for courage, Doug acknowledged. The Devil Dust addict jerked up his Mac-10. Aguilar caught the motion and gave a violent sweep of his arm to forestall his underling. Reluctantly, the Devil Duster lowered the assault weapon. His face was still crazed. Aguilar confronted Tyler.

Past the two men, Doug could see Ellen staring at him with despairing hope. He gritted his teeth in silence.

"What is your business here?" Aguilar's tone had grown angry.

"I'm Professor Dickinson Tyler of Oklahoma State University," Tyler announced indignantly. "This is my assistant, Ellen Rogers. We're here on an official archaeological survey authorized by the Peruvian government. These thugs grabbed us without provocation. We have no interest in whatever it is you're doing here, but I demand to speak to those Indians. Do you realize that they are undoubtedly the surviving remnants of a tribe hitherto unknown to—"

"Shut up!" Aguilar cried.

Tyler subsided with a shocked expression.

Aguilar rounded toward Doug. "What do you know of these two?"

Doug started forward. He wanted to get close to the drug lord and his captives. Simon swung his Mac-10 to bear with casual, wordless menace. Doug stopped. "What he says is true," he told Aguilar. "They're harmless. If anything happens to them, there could be repercussions. Let them go. They're not hurting anything."

Aguilar snorted contemptuously at the advice. He glanced back at the captives. "The man is a fool," he decided. "But the girl might have uses. We cannot let them go, of course. The man will have to be killed, and then we shall see about the girl." He eyed Ellen lewdly.

Tyler's expression was one of shock and outrage. Ellen gave Doug a last stricken look. Simon had relaxed only a little, and Doug felt a certain grim fatalism. He was probably about to get himself killed, but he just might get Simon and then Aguilar with the first shots from his .45. After that, it would be a free-fire zone and the odds would be hard against him. He offered up a silent prayer.

Aguilar stepped clear of Tyler. Ellen's captor yanked her back. She turned on him furiously, but he twisted her arm in a single cruel movement that left her helpless on her knees. Aguilar's head snapped toward the Devil Dusted gunman. He opened his mouth to give the order.

"Now, wait just a minute," Tyler said.

Doug flexed his hand to go for the .45.

A shot cracked through the thin mountain air.

Doug glimpsed one of the pagan warriors spin about, blood showing scarlet on his pale skin. In a single movement Doug snatched out the .45. He thumb-flicked the safety as he drew. A remote sector of his mind registered that they had come under fire from some unknown source.

He swung the .45 up into a shooter's stance and took the gunman holding Ellen. The .45 thundered and kicked in his grip. The gunman was rocked backward. Ellen twisted free. At that same moment, a horde of ragged savages erupted from the surrounding rocks. Doug had a wild impression of ancient shotguns, battered rifles, and heavy machetes wielded by desperadoes like those he had fought in the bar.

"El Demonio!" Simon hissed in recognition.

Doug snapped a shot at Aguilar and knew he had missed. Simon's Mac-10 gave a stuttering roar as he opened up on the attackers. There were at least a score of them. Aguilar himself was scrambling for safety. The roar of the Devil Duster's gun joined that of Simon's.

"Run!" Doug yelled at Ellen. He waved an arm toward the path into the valley. It was the only route open to them. He had no desire to be caught in the midst of a battle between these opposing factions.

Ellen heard him. She caught at the bemused Tyler's arm and began to drag him toward the rim of the plateau. Doug ran to join them.

The formation of warriors was dissolving. Some of them rushed forward to do battle. Others scattered into the rocks. A bellowing war cry sent echoes crashing from the mountain peaks. Cortozca charged the attackers. His massive club spun in his hands like the blade of a Japanese fencing master. Doug saw the foremost desperado swept completely off his feet by the whirling club. His broken body was flung aside.

Aguilar had swung a wicked Uzi assault gun from under his poncho and brought it into play. Shotgun and rifle blasts merged with the roars of the automatic weapons.

Doug reached the pathway at the same time as Tyler and Ellen. "Go on!" he shouted, and pivoted to trigger the .45. The desperado rushing upon them with a blazing antique revolver spun down onto his back. Doug ducked as a stray shot from somewhere snapped overhead. He plunged down the steep slope after Tyler and Ellen.

The steeply sloping side of the plateau was a jumble of upthrusting rocks. He caught Ellen's backward glance. It held a desperate, wordless plea for guidance. From the corner of his vision he glimpsed a flash of pale skin among the rocks to his left. No sanctuary was to be had there.

"That way!" He jabbed a pointing finger to their right. Ellen obeyed at once, and dodged out of view. Tyler followed her after a glance at Doug over his shoulder.

Doug swung about to cover their rear. He half slid, half ran backward down the slope. Gunfire and yells arose. He realized that the conflict was rapidly becoming a pitched battle among the rocks on the plateau's side. The warriors and Aguilar's men had apparently fallen back to cover beneath the assault of the desperadoes, who had pursued them with bloodthirsty tenacity.

A rifle cracked, and Doug saw Aguilar's young shotgun-bearer lurch erect and then fall. His body slid down the slope, accompanied by a small landslide. Doug had a chance for a shot at the desperado who had killed the youth. He didn't take it. Beyond, he saw another desperado stomping an unconscious warrior with methodical brutality. The bandit's face was twisted in primitive savagery. Doug went on. He ducked under the protection of a massive slab tilted against an outcropping. Tyler and Ellen were crouched there. Both ends of the shelter were open.

Ellen had the sense to keep quiet, but Tyler gripped Doug's shoulder with a surprisingly powerful hand. "Just what is all this?" he asked.

Doug was forced to admire his aplomb, even as he mentally berated the man's naïveté. He shrugged off Tyler's grip. "Everybody's trying to kill everybody else," he said. "We need to stay down. Are either of you armed, by any chance?"

"Of course not!"

"Great."

The sounds of battle were drawing closer. A man shouted from nearby, and a pump shotgun roared three times in quick succession. Someone began to scream.

"We need to get out of here," Doug decided aloud. Below them was the cloaking blanket of mist that hid the valley floor. "Work your way down," he ordered. "We should be able to slip away in that fog."

He seemed to have fully accepted his role as their nursemaid, he reflected drily. He wondered if his mission was irrevocably blown or if there was some way he might still salvage it. But that would have to wait, he thought as he heard Cortozca's barbaric battle cry echo among the rocks. He supposed that it spelled the death of yet another bandit. For now the mission could wait. He needed to concentrate on survival.

He spared a glance over his shoulder. Tyler and Ellen had left the shelter and were descending the slope quickly, staying to cover where possible. They moved well for amateurs. He might have expected it of Ellen, but Tyler continued to surprise him.

The scrape of a shoe on stone warned him. He turned his head sharply back toward the front entrance to the recess. As a figure pivoted into view there, Doug had an instant's perception of the wild face and flaming eyes of Aguilar's Devil Dusted gunman. The Mac-10 in his hands raked a wild line of fire over Doug's crouching form. A leaden whip seemed to flail the stone above his head. Chips pelted him and ricochets screamed. If he'd been standing, he would have been cut in half.

He shoved his arms out to full extension. The .45 roared deafeningly in the recess. He pumped two shots square into the gunman's torso. The heavy slugs shook his target like a building in an earthquake. The gunman stayed on his feet. He swung the barrel of the Mac-10 back to bear on Doug.

Doug emptied the clip into him—three more shots full on. He saw the gunman reel back beneath the hammering impacts. The wild yellow fire in his eyes never dimmed. The slide of Doug's .45 locked open on the empty clip.

Incredibly, the gunman lurched forward. Horror surged up in Doug. He saw the assault gun's barrel swing once more toward him. His thumb hit the clip release on the side of the .45. The empty magazine dropped free. Before it touched the ground, Doug's left hand snatched a second clip from the back pocket of his jeans. He slapped it into the butt of the .45 and thumbed the slide release. The renewed roar of the .45 drove the gunman staggering back. But he would not go down. The barrel of the Mac-10 quested blindly.

The horror rode Doug. Three more times he pulled the trigger. The glow faded from the demoniacal eyes. All at once the gunman collapsed as if he had been yanked to the floor.

Doug tried to cover the motionless form. For a moment the .45 would not hold still in his hands. The gunman didn't move. Nine shots, Doug calculated numbly. In the grip of the Devil Dust, the gunman had been virtually unstoppable.

Crouching, he backed away. He slipped out of the rear of the recess and moved swiftly down the slope. The first streamers of the curious mist brushed his face as he descended. Its touch was moist and warm. It smelled vaguely of sulphur. Some type of volcanic phenomenon, he guessed.

The temperature and humidity rose as he went down. Soon he felt as though he were passing through the interior of a sun-heated cloud. The diaphanous haze muffled the sounds of combat behind him. He had the sudden unnerving sensation of wandering disembodied through the mists of limbo.

"Doug!" The low-voiced call snapped him out of his reverie. He spotted the dim shapes of Ellen and Tyler crouched at the base of a massive boulder.

"You both okay?" he asked. His voice sounded muffled in the shrouding fog.

Ellen nodded. "Yes, we're all right." She was out of breath.

"I demand that you explain all this!" Tyler snapped.

"I think we're in the middle of some sort of longstanding feud. I don't know where the bandits came from, but I think their leader calls himself El Demonio."

"The Demon," Ellen whispered.

"You seem to know a great deal," Tyler said accusingly.

Doug stared hard at him. Tyler didn't flinch.

"Those men you were with," Ellen cut in hurriedly. "You were making a deal with them, weren't you?"

"Yes, but it's not what it seems. Will you trust me on that?"

She studied him earnestly. "You saved our lives," she said softly. "Of course I'll trust you."

Suddenly, Doug was intensely aware of her disheveled loveliness. Tyler was a scowling presence at her back.

Doug spun to his feet. He didn't know what had warned him, but he knew something had found them.

The warriors appeared to materialize from the fog. Their pale skin seemed to merge with it. Stone war clubs poised, a quartet of them confronted Doug from a dozen feet away. His grip was tight on the butt of the .45. He had a chance even against four.

Feet shuffled behind him. Ellen gasped. He glanced quickly. Tyler and Ellen were each helpless in the grip of a warrior. Stone knives menaced their throats. Doug swallowed hard. He looked back at the four club men. He still might win the fight, but his newly acquired wards would not survive it.

Carefully he bent down to place the .45 on the hard stone. Then he raised his hands. "We surrender," he said in Quechua.

Chapter Three

"It's unbelievable," Tyler said. "They have an entire civilization hidden here."

The thick layer of humid fog was above them like a ceiling. They had passed through it as they descended. It would conceal the entire valley and its contents from aerial observation, Doug noted.

On the valley floor below them was a village of rough stone houses. Some of them were two stories in height and looked spacious. A tundralike plain, cloaked with sparse greenery, stretched away down the valley on one side of the village. The valley was over a mile in length and at least half that in width.

Their captors urged them on down the hazardous path. None of these warriors had been with Cortozca on the plateau. They must have ascended from the village to investigate the combat. Doug wondered how many more of them there were.

The village was settled at the base of a mountain peak that overhung it ominously. The overhang would further conceal it from the air. In the face of the mountain was the enormous gaping black mouth of a cave. Doug guessed that a ten-story building could have been placed in it with room to spare. The interior of the cave was a wall of darkness.

Fur-clad women worked beside the stone houses of the village. Children played in the narrow streets. Older youths attended llamas grazing on the plain. Doug estimated that the village would house several hundred inhabitants. Everyone in sight had the same distinctive pale skin.

Doug glanced at Tyler. The professor's face carried a rapt expression of wonder as he gazed upon the village. Ellen, too, seemed fascinated, almost to the point of forgetting their peril. She and Tyler contrived to murmur excitedly to each other as they were escorted into the village. Doug scowled and studied the strange hamlet.

There was little sign of wood being used in construction. Nor did wooden utensils appear to be in evidence. Trees were sparse in this climate. Perhaps that accounted for the stone weaponry of the warriors and the predominant use of stone for utilitarian and construction purposes.

The inhabitants of the village paused in their activities to observe the arrival of the party. Doug saw a few elderly men and women as well as a scattering of additional warriors.

In front of a long, low building the party halted. Doug and his companions were ushered unceremoniously into a bare room. Whatever the culture, some things were always the same, Doug reflected grimly. He had no trouble recognizing this place for what it was—a cell.

"Wait just a moment," Tyler predictably began to protest. His Quechua was as fluent as Doug's.

The warriors ignored him, and the heavy stone door was pushed shut. Small windows near the ceiling were the only source of illumination.

Immediately Doug fell to examining the door. Tyler paced restlessly. Ellen watched first one of them and then the other, as if deciding which to join.

Doug's examination proved fruitless. Escape was impossible. He observed Tyler's ceaseless prowling. "What do you know about this tribe?" he asked.

It was as if he had flipped a switch. Tyler pivoted toward him. His face burned with a scholar's intense passion for his subject. "They are direct descendants of the tribe whose existence I have long postulated," he declared. "Obviously, they have remained isolated in this valley since the fall of the Incas. Thus, their bloodline has remained pure. The volcanic fog that covers this valley has prevented their existence from being observed by aerial surveys of this region. Their isolation and evident clannishness, coupled with this remote location, have likewise served to conceal their presence from anthropologists and archaeologists."

"Have you suspected their existence?" Doug asked.

Tyler shook his head sharply. "Not as an extant

culture. Ellen and I were looking for evidence of their past existence, such as artifacts or ruins."

"And we found traces of ruins on the plateau," Ellen added eagerly.

"That's correct. There was little left, but the indications were of a fairly advanced civilization. Their current use of the Quechua language indicates that they were once a subject race of the Incas, or at least highly influenced by them." His high brow furrowed. "For some reason, their culture has deteriorated over the centuries. Perhaps it was a result of the collapse of the Incas under the Spanish conquest. There's no way to tell as yet."

"The fog could also account for their pale pigmentation," Ellen contributed. She sounded almost like her mentor. "It must shield them from the worst of the sun's ultraviolet rays. Over the generations that have elapsed, the paleness of the skin has become characteristic of their race."

Tyler nodded agreement. "Do you realize that this will assure your doctorate, Ellen?"

Doug became aware he was frowning. "What do you know about their culture?" he asked before Tyler could go any further in his planning of Ellen's graduate education.

"Very little, actually," Tyler answered. "I've long suspected their contemporaneous existence with the Incas. Mention of them is found in the folklore of this region, in obscure reports made by some of the Spaniards themselves, and even in fragments of the Inca writings that have survived. What information I have gleaned from these sources indicates that they were most likely a matriarchy ruled by a succession of queens lineally descended from prehistoric times. They placed great stock in individual prowess in combat." Tyler's lips curled in distaste. "The queen's bodyguard, and sometimes her consort and mate, was always the tribe's mightiest warrior. His traditional title was that of the Queen's Warrior."

"Cortozca," Doug murmured.

"What?" Ellen asked.

"The Queen's Warrior," Doug elaborated. "That's what Aguilar called Cortozca, the leader of the warriors who were there when you were captured."

She nodded. "And Aguilar," she added hesitantly, "he was the boss of those men you were dealing with." Her eyes were intent on his face.

Doug nodded slowly. His eyes met hers. Clearly, she was still bothered by what she understood to be his means of livelihood. But old habits and patterns of survival were too deeply ingrained for him to discard them even now. He did not offer any further explanation. After a moment she turned away.

"Amazing." Tyler's tone was musing. He seemed to have missed their byplay. "The tradition of the Queen's Warrior has survived down through the centuries."

Another memory prodded Doug. "What about their religion?" he queried, because the more information he had about their captors, the better off he was.

"Apparently their religion centered around the volcanic activity in this area, although I can't be certain of any details."

"What about a God of the Dark Waters?"

Tyler frowned thoughtfully. "No. I've never heard of such a deity."

Briefly, Doug recounted Cortozca's use of the term.

"That's strange," Tyler said. He studied Doug dubiously. "Are you sure you understood correctly?"

Doug felt like a student being accused of inattention. "I understood." His tone made angry sparks flash in Tyler's dark eyes.

"I see," the professor said slowly. He drew himself up. "Perhaps it's time that Ellen and I understood some things as well. For example, the exact nature of your business here."

"Part of my business up on that plateau was saving your necks," Doug shot back. Maybe Tyler had not missed that subtle byplay between him and Ellen, after all.

"Whether or not you saved our lives is open to question, as are your purposes in being in this country at all." Tyler's tone was hard, his words precise. "What is not open to question is the fact that, by following your orders, we have ended up here as prisoners!"

"Dick! That's not fair!" Ellen stepped forward angrily. As she had done in the bar, she thrust herself between the two men. "Doug did save our lives," she spoke up to Tyler's imposing height. A pleading note had been added to her tone, and Doug did not like it. "And you're judging him without knowing all the facts. There may be circumstances we don't know about that could lead to an entirely different conclusion. Possibly, there are things Doug can't tell us for reasons of his own."

Doug saw the way her face lit up with the justness of her cause. Tyler actually retreated a step. Clearly he was unhappy at her siding with Doug. "Perhaps you're right," he conceded reluctantly. He looked past her at Doug. "We will let the matter of your purposes here pass for the moment." His tone sharpened. "But, Mr. Bonner, or whatever your real name is, you have an unfortunate tendency to resort to violence before it is absolutely certain that there's no other recourse. Violence is degrading, and frequently the results are irrevocable. It has been my experience that a man of intellect and learning can frequently avoid violence, even in potentially violent situations, through diplomacy and the judicious assertion of reason."

Doug shook his head. Disputing with Tyler was pointless. But he was unwilling to let the matter rest without at least an effort at rebuttal. "The violence *is* degrading. I won't argue that," he said flatly. "What's even more degrading is standing by and letting violence be done to yourself or to others and not

taking action to stop it. The results of that can be irrevocable too. Sometimes, violence can be met only
by violence. I don't choose it, but when it's forced
on me, I deal with it."

"You seem to have a propensity for doing so,"
Tyler said.

"You'd better thank God that I do." Doug turned
away to end the pointless debate. He crossed to the
far end of the cell. He was conscious of a whispered
exchange between Ellen and Tyler behind him. He
could not make out the words. He gazed up at a small
window. It was too high for him to see out of unless
he chinned himself up to it.

"I'm sorry," Ellen's voice said behind him.

He turned and found that she had moved very
close to him. It surprised him that he had not heard
or sensed her nearness.

"Dick didn't mean everything that he said. He's
high-strung, and he's used to being in charge."

Doug resisted the impulse to ask if Tyler was in
charge of *her*. He already knew that the answer was
no. "You might remind him that he's not in his classroom here," he said instead. "The players all make
their own rules, and the winners are the ones who
survive."

She shuddered. "This is all so awful. Can we ever
get away from here?"

"We'll have a chance at some point."

"You mean if they don't kill us first?"

"Something like that."

She shuddered again. Then she seemed to reassert control over her emotions. "It's funny," she said. "Under other circumstances, I'd have given a year of my life for the opportunity to see this place, much less be one of the members of the scientific community to discover it. Proving the existence of this race has become a kind of obsession with Dick. And, since I've been working with him, I've grown interested in it too."

"You were in his classes at the university?" Doug was careful to keep his tone neutral.

As she nodded, Doug glimpsed the same scholar's passion he had seen in Tyler. "My major was archaeology," she told him. "I concentrated on biblical archaeology in my undergraduate work. Then, when I got into Dick's classes as part of my master's program, I became fascinated with his work. He's internationally acclaimed, you know."

Doug nodded to keep her talking.

"Dick saw I was interested, and he encouraged me. He's been very good to me. He chose me as his research assistant over dozens of other applicants, and he arranged for me to accompany him on this trip. He's been a perfect gentleman." She looked quickly away, as if suddenly aware that she had volunteered the information on their personal relationship.

Doug bit back a response. Her relationship with Tyler was none of his business. Still, he felt a curious relief at her revelation.

From outside the window came the sounds of a

commotion. Something was happening out in the street. Again Doug looked up at the window, gauging its height. He supposed that the commotion had to do with the recent battle on the plateau.

"Boost me up," Ellen said, and she put both hands on his shoulders and lifted a foot expectantly. "I'll see what's going on."

Doug had the absurd impulse to kiss her, but he cupped his hands and lifted as she placed her foot in them. She was surprisingly light.

She caught the edge of the window and took some of her weight. He held her feet in his palms as she peered out.

"There's a crowd gathering," she reported after a moment. "Wait a minute. It's the warriors from up on the plateau. They've come back. I can see the big one—Cortozca. He's the leader. And they have one of the bandits, or whatever they are, as prisoner. The townspeople don't seem to like the bandit." She paused. "Aguilar is with them."

"Is he a prisoner?"

"I don't think so. He's not tied up like the bandit."

Carefully he lowered her, holding her trim waist to steady her after she stepped out of his hands. Her palms came to rest on his shoulders. For a moment it was almost as if they were going to embrace. She lifted her hands and he released her reluctantly. She stepped back. He was breathing harder than the slight exertion warranted.

Doug told himself to think about what she had seen outside. "Where were they going?" he asked.

"Toward the cave."

Tyler had drawn near them. He seemed to have decided to disregard his earlier differences with Doug. Nor did he appear to have noticed anything untoward in Doug's lifting Ellen to the window. "The cave may be the site of their religious practices," he said. "I saw no sign of a temple in the village."

"Were there any of Aguilar's men with him?" Doug asked Ellen.

"One of them. The man who was closest to you on the plateau. They didn't have him tied, either."

"That would be Simon," Doug said grimly. So Aguilar and his chief gunman had survived. Doug didn't like the ramifications of their unrestrained presence.

He wondered about their own situation. True, they had not been bound like the desperadoes, but they had certainly not been given the run of the village, either. Was their fate even now being decided in the huge cave?

His question went unanswered for the next hour. Doug watched the slow crawl of the hands of his Consort diver's watch. He evaluated various scenarios for escape. Tyler slipped his miniature computer from its belt sheath and began a series of calculations. Neither the computer nor the walkie-talkie had been taken from him and Ellen by their captors.

The high-pitched fluting of the computer bounced irritatingly off the stone walls of the cell. Doug scowled but kept silent. Once, Tyler called Ellen to him and excitedly showed her the results of some computation. She listened and nodded, but did not appear particularly interested. She glanced briefly at Doug. When she left Tyler's side, she moved around the cell in slow circles, gazing up at the windows.

Muffled sounds outside the door drew their attention sharply. Doug rose to his feet and motioned Tyler and Ellen away from the door. They obeyed, Tyler grudgingly. Doug tensed as the door swung open. He did not know what moves to make. It all depended on timing and circumstances.

He relaxed slightly as they were ushered out of the cell by six warriors, clad and armed like their captors earlier. Doug noted that each of them bore the blue tattoo of some fanged reptilian beast on his forehead. The tattoo reminded him of the stone war clubs and their monstrous motif. Were these warriors part of some elite military sect?

They were escorted through the village toward the huge maw of the cave. Doug could not help the instinctive slowing of his steps as they drew near. Ellen moved closer beside him. The guards hustled them forward.

Doug looked up at the massive overhang thrusting out from the cliff face more than ten stories above. He had the sudden feeling that its immense weight might come crashing down upon them at any moment. A detached segment of his mind marveled at the superb natural camouflage of this place, which had concealed it from the outer world for centuries.

Ringed by warriors, they passed under the overhang and into the enormous black mouth of the cave.

"This is amazing!" Tyler exclaimed.

Ellen gasped. Doug could only stare at the bizarre alien world spread out before them. The entire mountain must be hollow to accommodate the vast spectacle within it. The chamber itself was enormous. Doug could not estimate how many acres it covered. The farthest limits were lost in darkness.

All around the periphery of the chamber were the ruins of an ancient stone city. Doug was reminded of the cliff dwellings of Arizona and New Mexico, although they were dwarfed by these present structures. The buildings seemed to have been literally carved from the stone walls of the cave. Some were several stories in height. All were flat roofed. Their scale and magnificence were stunning.

The architecture had a vague Inca motif. Wide stairways ascended stepped pyramidal structures. Carved images of pagan deities snarled silently. The black eyes of windows stared from the crumbling faces of the buildings. Obviously, the great stone city had long since been abandoned to neglect and disrepair. Some structures had collapsed into piles of rubble. Others had been badly eroded by natural geological processes within the cave. It had become a spirit city, haunted by the wraiths of its past grandeur.

In the center of the chamber was the dark surface of a great subterranean lake. It was half surrounded by the stone jungle of the city. Like the cavern itself, the lake's limits were lost in the void. Strange stirs and ripples disturbed its surface, as if it thrived with an unnatural life. He guessed from the cave's steamy humidity that the lake was volcanically heated.

And the cavern was not dark, Doug slowly realized. A faint, eerie luminescence cast a spectral glow off the swirling waters of the lake, and it highlighted the empty stone windows of the city. The light seemed to emanate from a section of the cavern wall and from part of the city itself.

Doug saw that some form of subterranean, phosphorescent vegetation had spread across almost a fourth of one side of the cavern wall and the attached buildings. Undoubtedly the process had taken centuries. The fungoid growth must have been spawned in the humid black recesses of the cave. Its luminescent qualities served now to spread a pale ghostly light across the huge cavern.

Doug became aware that their captors were leading them toward a pillared temple at the edge of the lake. Beside it was what appeared to be an enormous stone altar that towered far above a man's height. He was conscious of the silent, awed presences of Ellen and Tyler beside him. How much more spectacular and significant this lost underground world must be to them, with their knowledge of lost cultures and ancient civilizations.

As they drew near the temple, Doug saw the fanged reptilian motif of the war clubs and tattoos repeated in the carved stonework of the structure. He resisted the impulse to keep turning his head to stare about him at the wonders of the bizarre cave world.

Up flat stone steps they were escorted. They passed through a wide lintelled doorway and into the temple. Bracketed torches lit a broad hallway. At its end, they emerged into a large room where two stone thrones were set atop a two-level dais. Upon the higher throne sat a woman.

Doug was struck first by her beauty. The characteristic pale skin of her race gave her a translucent, glacial loveliness that was heightened by her statuesque form. Even her seated position could not obscure the perfection of her figure. She wore a supple fur garment like a leotard and a cape that flowed down around her. Snowy blond hair fell to brush her strong, bare shoulders. Her legs were long and sleek, ending in almost dainty sandaled feet.

Looking up at her face, Doug saw a compassion and intelligence that softened the almost cold lines of her classical beauty. Only the fullness of her face reflected the usual broad Indian features. She occupied the throne with a regal ease.

Standing just behind her, powerful arms folded, was Cortozca. He towered above her like a colossus of stone. Firelight from wall-mounted braziers cast flickering shadows that defined his musculature. As his dark eyes locked with Doug's, Doug read an irrational hostility. Together, Cortozca and the woman presented a scene of barbaric magnificence.

The man in the lower throne had the sharp features of a stoic philosopher. His head was a high, shaved dome. Light from the flames seemed to reflect a smoldering yellow glow in his eyes. His lean, sinewy body was clad in a loincloth and cape. His gaunt chest was covered by a blue tattoo of the familiar fanged reptile.

Wariness prickled the hair at the nape of Doug's neck as he saw the fourth person on the dais. Still in his colorful poncho, sneering just a little, Salvador Aguilar seemed right in place in these demonic surroundings.

Doug had only moments to speculate as to what unholy alliance Aguilar had formed with these barbaric rulers. Their escort of warriors withdrew slightly, leaving Doug and his companions standing before the woman. In the dim shadows behind the dais, Doug saw a cordon of other armed warriors. Half of them had the reptilian tattoo on their foreheads.

"I grant you entry to Quaztar," the woman said in the oddly accented Quechua. Her tone was calm. The words were obviously part of some formality.

Doug started to speak. He sensed Tyler doing the same.

"No," the woman cut them off imperiously. "She will speak for you." Her extended finger was pointed at Ellen.

"We are honored to be here," Ellen said with proper humility. She seemed to accept her responsibility as spokesperson with casual aplomb.

The woman on the throne nodded, as if approving of Ellen's response. Doug did not miss the quick glance exchanged between Cortozca and the man on the lower throne. He wondered what sort of intrigues slithered beneath this facade of pageantry.

"I am Tanztra," the woman said to Ellen. She virtually ignored Doug and Tyler. "This place is Quaztar, and I am its Queen."

A matriarchy indeed, Doug thought. And this queen was obviously not a figurehead. But he could still sense rival political factions subtly at odds here.

"I'm Ellen Rogers," Ellen responded to the Queen's introduction. She indicated Doug and Tyler by name. "We were brought here by your warriors."

Tanztra's nod was sharp. "I have received reports of what occurred." Her glance somehow seemed to slide to Cortozca behind her. "Although, perhaps, they are not full reports. Tell me what took place."

Ellen hesitated, then spoke firmly. "Dick and I are scholars. We had come a long way to these mountains as part of our studies. The followers of this man"—she indicated Aguilar on the lower platform of the dais—"captured us without reason. We would have been killed. When the fighting broke out, Doug saved us. We were attempting to escape the fighting when your warriors found us."

The Queen drew the tip of her finger from her

lower lip, down across her chin, and along the sleek column of her neck in a reflective gesture. She studied Ellen, then shifted her gaze to Tyler and Doug. Her dark eyes lingered on Doug.

Ellen took a tiny step forward. "Queen Tanztra," she said boldly, "why is this man, Aguilar, here? He is an evil man."

Doug didn't breathe.

"It is not your place to question, Ellen," Tanztra said silkily. There was no heat in her tone. "The Lord Aguilar has been chosen as Chief Counsel by Mixtek, the High Priest of the God of the Dark Waters." She nodded with studied calm at the man on the other throne.

Mixtek's lean body stiffened. The beast stenciled on his chest appeared to spread its fanged jaws wider as the wiry muscles bunched and flexed. "How does this woman dare to question and malign my Chief Counsel?" he demanded harshly.

"She did not know of his status when she spoke," Tanztra brushed the protest aside.

Mixtek's eyes flared like those of a Devil Dust addict. They flicked searchingly to Cortozca. Aguilar had lost his sneer.

Doug was beginning to comprehend some of the opposing forces at play here. Mixtek, the High Priest, and Cortozca, the Queen's Warrior, were obviously allied against the Queen. The tattooed warriors were a part of some military branch attached to the priesthood and probably loyal to Mixtek. Doug wondered how many of the other warriors were loyal to the Queen.

As a newcomer and confederate of Cortozca, Aguilar had been seized for use as some kind of pawn in the subtle struggle and been given a title to legitimatize his position. It was political maneuvering as old as mankind, Doug reflected, but none the less dangerous because of it. Aguilar's presence was a wild card that, he sensed, somehow threatened to tip the balance of power. But Aguilar was a dangerous man to use as a pawn. Having an official position would suit him, since he undoubtedly was scheming to obtain greater access to the source of the Devil Dust.

"Interlopers are rare here," Tanztra told Ellen. "We have maintained our isolation over the centuries by strict enforcement of certain laws. One of these is that interlopers, once they enter or see Quaztar, are not permitted to leave."

Ellen was pale. "We are in your power, Queen," she said.

Tanztra nodded. "Quite so." She appraised the High Priest and his newfound Counsel. "Remaining here does not imply a sentence of death. It is another of our laws that, just as the High Priest may name even an interloper as his Chief Counsel, so may I, as Queen, name a young woman as my confidante and adviser by granting her the title of Queen's Maiden. I so name you, Ellen Rogers."

"I accept," Ellen said promptly. "These two men

are my warriors and bodyguards. I ask your protection of them."

Tanztra gave her regal nod. "Granted." The entire exchange might have been planned, Doug thought, so great was the obvious rapport between the two women.

"No!" Mixtek found voice at last.

"You object, High Priest?" Tanztra inquired with an arched eyebrow. "On what grounds? The position of Queen's Maiden is an ancient and respected one, at least as old as that of Chief Counsel to the High Priest. And, likewise, it is not barred to interlopers."

Mixtek sank back into his throne. His lean features were like the cutting edge of one of the stone daggers. The tattooed beast on his chest heaved as if in baffled anger. Tanztra looked back at Ellen. A faint smile touched the Queen's lips.

Her move had been a shrewd one, Doug calculated, and Ellen had had the savvy to play it hard to their advantage. He marveled at the instant affinity that had sprung up between the pair.

By naming Ellen to an official capacity, Tanztra had apparently countered whatever political advantage Mixtek and Cortozca had gained by bringing Aguilar into their ranks. Doug couldn't begin to fathom the full ramifications of what had happened, but he sensed that they, too, were now pawns in this game of politics.

Aguilar had leaned forward to whisper in Mixtek's ear. The drug lord straightened. "The two men are enemies of my Counsel, and, therefore, of me," the High Priest declared. "They cannot claim the favor of the Queen's Maiden."

Aguilar's expression was sadistically triumphant. Apparently he had not missed the fact that Doug had killed at least one of his men as well as taken a shot at Aguilar himself during the battle on the plateau. Whatever came of this convoluted rivalry, Doug guessed that his cover with Aguilar was blown.

"These men are the warriors of the Queen's Maiden," Tanztra told Mixtek. "Therefore, they are entitled to my protection."

"With respect, my Queen," Cortozca spoke for the first time, "they cannot claim the title of warrior until they have passed the Proving."

Tanztra swiveled sharply in her throne to look up at the giant warrior. "They are interlopers," she objected. "They could not survive the Proving. You cannot require it of them!"

"With respect, my Queen, I can," Cortozca replied smoothly. "To be a warrior of Quaztar, a man must first undergo the Proving of the Warriors."

Tanztra shot Ellen a look that said she had somehow failed her new adviser. Once again she drew her fingertip down her chin and along her neck. Her beautiful features betrayed the same underlying disturbance as the waters of the dark lake.

Ellen cut a look at Doug. Now he felt an affinity

between her and him. He gave her a slight nod. "My warriors will face the Proving," she announced.

Behind the Queen, Cortozca smiled with evil satisfaction. "Let the proving ground be prepared," he commanded.

Chapter Four

"**I**t was all I could do," Ellen insisted. "It gives both of you a chance to survive and escape."

"It was foolish," Tyler said coldly. "You have committed us to an unknown and undoubtedly hazardous ordeal with no advance knowledge of the risks."

"Give her a break, Tyler," Doug told him. "She probably saved our lives. You ought to be complimenting her on being sharp enough to act when she had the chance."

Tyler rounded sharply on him. Behind the professor, Doug caught Ellen's look of gratitude. They were in the small temple room where they had been secured following the pressured audience before Quaztar's rulers. Soon, he and Tyler would have to face the Proving of the Warriors.

"Extricating us from our circumstances requires careful and rational planning," Tyler snapped, "not impulsive and emotional decisions. Further, your violent propensities will not help us in the long run."

"Maybe not," Doug said, "but they might keep us alive for now. Look, once we get out on this proving ground, stay close to me. I'll try to watch out for you and give you a hand."

Tyler unleashed a look of unspeakable contempt. "That will hardly be necessary."

Doug shrugged. "Suit yourself. The offer still stands." He turned and crossed to the far side of the small room. He should be praying for strength instead of arguing with the pompous fool, he thought bitterly.

"Don't be too hard on Dick," Ellen said. Once again she had approached noiselessly.

He turned to her. "Quit apologizing for him!" The words were more harsh than he had intended.

She flinched. "You're right," she acknowledged. "I shouldn't have to defend him, should I?"

Doug didn't answer. He looked past her to Tyler's dark, brooding figure in the far corner. He hoped the professor and his amateur's naïveté wouldn't be too much of a liability in whatever lay ahead.

"Thank you for what you said about the way I handled things with Tanztra," Ellen's voice intruded. She was gazing intently at him. "It's like she's my big sister. I could almost understand her before she spoke."

"You did fine," Doug assured her.

She looked down quickly, as if flustered by her thoughts. Then her eyes came resolutely back.

"Aguilar said you were his enemy." Her voice was still hesitant. "Is that true?"

Doug nodded. He felt a sense of having a burden lifted from him. "I always was. He just didn't know it until I shot his hired gun and took a shot at him."

"You're some kind of undercover agent, aren't you?"

"Yeah," Doug admitted. The barriers came down at last. "After high school I spent a year with the local police force in my hometown. Then I joined the Drug Enforcement Agency." *From high school sports hero as captain of the baseball team to undercover agent in two easy career moves,* he thought.

Her face lit up joyfully. "I just knew you couldn't really be a part of anything that awful, no matter how it seemed or what Dick said." She laid a hand on his chest. He could feel the warmth of her touch through his shirt. "I'm glad you told me," she said softly.

Doug didn't plan it. He took her shoulders and kissed her quickly on the lips. She stepped back in surprise as he released her.

"I—" she began.

The working of the door's crude lock from outside halted her. Doug glimpsed the pale, strained face of Tyler turned toward them from the far corner. He realized that the professor had seen the impulsive kiss.

The door opened wide enough to admit a single warrior. Doug saw that he did not carry the evil tattoo of the minions of Mixtek.

"I am Dalzar," he greeted them hurriedly. "I am Chief Warrior of the Queen's Guards. She sent me to you. We do not have much time." He turned and made a slight formal nod of obeisance to Ellen.

So there were warriors loyal to the Queen, Doug reflected. And they would be formidable opponents, if Dalzar was any indication.

"Can you tell us about the Proving of the Warriors?" Doug asked. Tyler drew near as he spoke.

"The Queen wanted me to warn you," Dalzar said. "In some of the phases of the Proving you will engage in personal combat with various opponents. The combats are not intended to be to the death, but the Queen suspects that there may be treachery. Some of the warriors participating in the combats will be loyal to Mixtek and Cortozca. You must be wary of them. They may not abide by the law, which requires that the lives of those being proved be spared, if possible, even if they do not pass the Proving."

"That figures," Doug said. He remembered Cortozca's arrogant and confident smile.

"The Queen cannot intercede," Dalzar went on. "I tried to obtain a place among the participating warriors, but Cortozca rejected me. He knows where my loyalties lie."

"Exactly how will this Proving be conducted?" Tyler spoke up.

"There are four phases. In the first, you must pass safely through the Chamber of Whispering Death. Total silence is required for you to survive. In the second phase, you will be pursued by warriors across the Great Plain. If caught, you are to be subdued by the pursuing warriors although not killed. The third phase is the crossing of the Abyss of Flame. Once across, you must match your skills against warriors in single combat."

"Quite a picnic," Doug commented. He saw that Ellen's face looked strained. He felt a little strained himself.

"The true attributes of a warrior are these." Cortozca was apparently reciting a formal opening to the Proving. "Stealth, endurance, courage, and fighting skills. To be a Warrior of Quaztar, a man must prove himself and demonstrate that he possesses the true attributes of a warrior. See there the Chamber of Whispering Death, where your stealth will be tested." He pointed.

Doug looked toward the black mouth of a cave branching off from the main cavern housing the ruined city and the subterranean lake. He and Tyler had been given stone torches with the ends hollowed to hold flammable oil. The flame emerged through a small hole. The crude stone lamps would provide illumination. Tyler gripped his torch with a steady hand. His face, in the light of its flame, was determined.

Accompanied by a retinue of blue-tattooed warriors, Cortozca and the High Priest stood as if in judgment over prisoners of war. Doug glimpsed

Aguilar's smirking face. Simon lurked at his master's back.

Ellen and Tanztra were also backed by a group of warriors, with Dalzar at their head. The Queen's face was like an image carved from ice. Doug wondered what had kept open warfare from erupting long ago between the two factions. The balance of power must be equal for the uneasy peace to have held this long.

"The Chamber emerges onto the Great Plain," Cortozca told them. His voice echoed. "Should you survive, we will be awaiting you there for the next phase. Do not attempt to turn back once you have entered the Chamber."

Ellen left Tanztra's side and hurried to them. Her eyes were bright with tears.

"I'll be praying," she whispered, then tiptoed quickly to kiss Doug on the lips. He felt the brief pressure of her hands on his chest.

Tyler turned coldly away from her. She hesitated. "Be careful, Dick," she said almost timidly to his back.

Tyler looked around at her, but made no other acknowledgment of her words or presence. She glanced again at Doug. Troubled emotions conflicted on her face. Doug could still taste the quick press of her lips. He managed a nod of reassurance. Reluctantly, she withdrew to Tanztra's side. Doug saw the Queen reach briefly to clasp her hand comfortingly.

"The Proving of the Warriors begins!" Cortozca's voice rose to a shout.

A half dozen of the High Priest's followers escorted Doug and Tyler forward past crumbling ruins towering against the cavern walls. As they neared the cave mouth, the warriors lagged back and then stopped completely. One of them pointed in a solemn silence. Doug glanced at Tyler. Tyler did not meet his gaze. Torch uplifted, he started forward. Doug followed.

They halted at the cave mouth. Neither had spoken. Doug's extended torch revealed a subterranean gallery littered with the rubble of fallen stalactites. Overhead, like the fangs of some gargantuan beast whose maw they faced, intact stalactites pointed downward. There was no sign of danger.

Stealth, Doug thought. *Absolute silence. What enemy lurks, silent and unseen, within?*

He started forward. Tyler's abruptly extended arm blocked his way. Doug looked at him inquiringly. Without speaking, Tyler bent and picked up a fragment of masonry. He tossed it far into the chamber.

Almost simultaneously with the echoing clatter of its impact among the rubble, a massive stalactite split away from the ceiling with a ripping crack of sound. It plunged down to smash itself to fragments on the littered floor. The rebounding echoes brought a dozen smaller spires clattering down. The sounds of their falling, heightened by some freakish acoustic effect, seemed to physically buffet Doug. Slowly he turned his head to look once more at Tyler. The man had almost certainly saved his life.

Tyler's nostrils flared. "I surmised as much," he whispered with an edge of triumph. "The geological structure is extremely fragile. Too much noise could bring down the entire ceiling. We must be extremely careful to avoid any sharp sounds."

Whispering death, indeed, Doug thought. This bizarre natural phenomenon was as dangerous as any living opponent they might face.

Cautiously he edged forward. The floor of the gallery was strewn with the countless debris of past falls. It would make normal walking impossible. Doug stepped gingerly over a cylindrical section of stalactite and entered the chamber itself. In the uncertain light of the torch, his eyes searched the floor ahead. The slightest misstep, the turning of a foot on an unseen stone, could end the Proving in these earliest stages of the first phase.

He was conscious of Tyler moving with surprising skill behind him. He could hear the other man's breathing. His own breath seemed thunderous in his ears.

The torchlight illuminated a wide passageway ahead of them. Doug placed his feet as if he were attempting to walk on quicksand. He was careful to avoid treading on any of the loose debris underfoot. He had to sidestep to avoid a stalagmite higher than his head. He eased his way under a leaning pillar of stone that had toppled against it.

Pellets of ice seemed to be condensing on his forehead. He blinked against tears from the heat of the torch and the constant strain of staring at the shadowed floor before them. How far had they come? he wondered. He didn't want to look back. Overhead, the points of the stalactites glinted in the torchlight.

A gleam of white caught his eye, and he paused to extend his torch toward it. Impaled by a fallen stalactite, a human skeleton lay sprawled grotesquely on the floor. Doug drew his torch back. At least one earlier candidate had not made it through. Tyler hissed at him to move on.

A small hill of fragments blocked their path. Doug skirted it, having to mount its uneven slope. He tested each step before putting his weight down. The fragments shifted fractionally under his feet. Unthinkingly he thrust out his hand to brace himself. He felt a stone the size of a football come loose at his touch and start to fall. Convulsively his fingers tightened about it. The muscles bunched in his forearm. Carefully he laid the fragment aside.

His teeth were gritted as he eased clear of the hill's slope. He turned to assist Tyler. The human skull glared at him out of the rubble from less than a foot away. He recoiled in shock. He felt his foot kick hard against a loose fragment that clattered loudly away. The reverberating sound battered him as if he were trapped in a gigantic stone bell.

The cracking of stone sounded from overhead. A great mass plunged down upon him. Instinct shifted him fast sideways. The falling stalactite shattered itself where he had stood. It was as thick as his body.

He would have been impaled like the skeleton they had passed.

He locked himself into rigidity as the crashing echoes hammered the chamber walls. He was conscious of Tyler frozen precariously halfway over the slope of the small hill. A rain of smaller projectiles fell about them. Doug felt a flying chip scar his forehead. He flinched for fear of his eyes.

The echoes pursued themselves into silence. Doug turned his gaze on the sneering skull. A skeletal hand and forearm reaching to claw at the side of the hill were the only other parts of the skeleton that were visible. Doug realized that the victim must have been scrambling over a lesser version of the hill of rubble when some inadvertent sound had collapsed a good section of the ceiling atop him. Here was another entrant in the Proving who had never made it to the second phase.

Chilled, Doug turned to offer a hand to Tyler as the latter descended. Angrily, Tyler waved the gesture away. His glare was venomous. He motioned Doug forward.

Doug went on. At his feet a crack gaped in blackness. It was at least five feet wide. A fairly easy jump, but not when it had to be made without sound. The floor was too cluttered for any sort of running start.

He crouched and jumped. The slice of blackness flashed below him. He tensed his legs on landing, bending his knees to absorb the shock in a martial-arts technique for landing softly from a leaping kick.

His booted feet met stone with barely a whisper of sound.

He stepped away and turned as Tyler made the jump. His feet came down solidly on the stone but without an echo. For a moment Tyler teetered on the brink. His arms flailed. The torch fell from his grip. Doug shot out his hand. His fingers clamped on Tyler's hard wrist. He jerked. Tyler lurched forward and caught his balance. Doug glimpsed the flame of the torch falling endlessly away into darkness.

For a moment his face was close to Tyler's. Tyler snapped his wrist free from Doug's grip. Again he made his angry motion to proceed.

You're welcome, Doug thought savagely. Maybe they were even for his blunder back by the hill of fragments.

He restrained his anger as he pressed on. Ahead of him the darkness seemed to lessen. But he resisted the impulse to dash forward. After a few more steps, the passage began to turn. Daylight almost blinded him as he rounded the curve.

They emerged on the edge of the plain outside the village. The entire gathering from inside the main cavern awaited them. Doug saw Ellen start forward impulsively. Tanztra restrained her. The Queen's icy aloofness seemed to soften with relief as she saw they were unharmed.

Cortozca pointed imperiously across the valley. Apparently they were to have no respite. Doug looked out over the plain with its carpet of coarse grass. The herds of llamas and their tenders were no longer in evidence. Stripped to loincloths, a dozen unarmed warriors waited expectantly.

He might have underestimated the length of the valley earlier, he thought. From this perspective, it looked to be a full three miles to the distant mountains that formed a barrier at the valley's end. A good run. He hoped Tyler was up to it. The professor surprised him by stepping forward confidently.

He looked around as Doug joined him. "Stay clear of me, Bonner," he warned. "Your clumsiness almost got us killed in there."

Doug nodded at the waiting warriors. "They won't play easy with us if they catch us. Better pace yourself so you don't give out."

"I'm an experienced long-distance runner. I've taken part in marathons all over the United States."

"Congratulations. I hope you survive this one."

"I'll be waiting for you at the end, Bonner."

Tyler pushed off into the long, casual stride of a trained runner. Doug glanced one last time at the waiting pursuers. He thought of greyhounds straining to be unleashed after the live rabbits used in training. The rabbits never survived, they were torn to pieces. He set out in Tyler's wake.

He guessed that he was nowhere near the league in which Tyler fancied himself as a runner. The sparse grass underfoot was not a bad surface, but the air he drew into his lungs was thin and moist. The temperature in the valley was warmer than on the plateau. His body was drenched with sweat in minutes.

Ahead of him, Tyler ran with an easy economy of motion. Doug made no effort to overtake him. From behind came a bloodthirsty cry from a dozen throats. The pack had taken up the hunt.

Doug glanced back. They had a lead of over a hundred yards on their pursuers. Two of the warriors had drawn immediately ahead of their companions and were sprinting hard. Doug understood their tactics. Successive pairs of warriors would keep the pressure on, allowing the other members of the pack to hold a slower pace until they took their turns to sprint ahead.

Tyler's pace faltered slightly, then resumed. Doug guessed that the professor had not fully comprehended the harrowing strain of being pursued by relentless enemies out for blood. This was not quite like a run in the Boston Marathon, and the mental pressure could be as debilitating as the physical exertion.

Doug's own breath began to pump in his chest. He could feel the pull of his thigh muscles and the impacts of his feet traveling up through his legs. He started to count strides. At a hundred he looked back again—bad policy on a track but essential in this deadly race. The two sprinters had slowed and another pair had pulled ahead of the pack. He and Tyler still had a good lead, but it was lessening.

Tyler showed no further signs of tiring. They had covered a mile now, Doug judged. The mountains looked no closer. Tyler flung back a glance. The pace was beginning to tell on him, after all.

The plain stretched away endlessly before them. Doug's lungs swelled to pull in air to sustain his pumping legs. He had a sudden image of how they must look if viewed by some watcher from high overhead—two tiny figures racing desperately across the desolate flatland ahead of the ravening pack beneath a ceiling of fog. He knew that they would be unlikely to survive being overtaken by their pursuers.

He had lost track of his strides. He checked behind him again. Two fresh warriors had taken the lead. The gap had narrowed still more. He flung himself on. Two miles now. Surely they had covered two miles.

He glimpsed the pale muscular figure as it launched itself up from the grass at Tyler. A stone dagger thrust at his chest. Tyler turned awkwardly in midstride to meet the attack. The blade went harmlessly past him. He grappled ineffectually with his opponent.

An assassin, Doug's mind flashed. Cortozca had not trusted the pursuing warriors to do the job. He had set this killer here to await them.

Doug turned his rushing momentum into a twisting leap. His left leg tucked under his hurtling form. His right leg snapped out straight. His foot smashed against the attacking warrior's shoulder. It spun him away from Tyler.

Doug landed as lightly as he had in the cave. Tyler

staggered against him. He thrust the professor reeling away, and then swiveled sideways to meet the warrior's rush. His kick had not hurt the assassin. The stone blade was still clenched in a pale fist. In moments, the first pair of pursuers would be upon them as well.

The assassin dived toward Doug, both feet leaving the ground. Doug had an instant's impression of his tattooed face. The dagger came at his throat like a projectile. He snapped his left arm up and out. Hard wrist met hard wrist. The dagger spun away. The warrior's full weight crashed into Doug. He was driven over backward. Falling, he slammed the heel of his palm up to the warrior's jaw. White teeth in the assassin's snarling mouth clicked sharply together. Doug twisted from beneath him as they hit the ground. He shifted up onto his side to chop down with a hand like an ax. Beneath him, he felt the warrior shudder into stillness.

Doug came crouching to his feet. The first pair of pursuers were scant yards away. One was ahead of the other. Tyler had caught his balance but had not moved. He looked bewildered, his arrogance stripped from him by the raw slash of violence.

"Go on!" Doug shouted. "I'll hold them off!"

He had time only to glimpse Tyler turning clumsily away. Then he spun as the first of the two warriors came to the attack. The long run and his sprint did not seem to have winded him. His moves were the fluid ones of some form of unarmed combat.

And it appeared to be an effective one. The flat of the warrior's naked foot rammed at Doug's chest. The man leaned far back as he executed the stamping kick. The full drive of his powerful leg was behind the technique.

Barely in time, Doug got his hands up to catch the driving foot, and with his arms flexed almost to his chest, he gripped the callused foot and twisted with all the strength in his shoulders. The warrior's body spun into an involuntary cartwheel. Doug reeled back a step in reaction. Suddenly he couldn't seem to breathe. He saw the second of the pair pulling up short as he neared the combatants.

The warrior he had thrown bounced back to his feet. He looked surprised. He spun toward Doug in a series of whirling turns. The edges of his open palms lashed at Doug with the momentum of his spinning body behind them. Doug dropped low and spun himself, his right leg extended. The open hands slashed over his head. His right leg swept around in an arc. It cut the warrior's legs cleanly from beneath him and he crashed to the ground. Still crouched low on one leg, Doug lifted his extended leg and hammered his heel down at the warrior's head. His body went limp.

Doug straightened. The remaining warrior was no longer blocked by his comrade. He came in fast. Doug saw the stone dagger he produced from his loincloth. Another of Cortozca's killers. Out on the plain, the pursuing pack raised barbaric cries of eagerness. They were closing fast now. Their prey was within their grasp.

The assassin lunged. He wanted to finish his bloody task quickly. Doug sidestepped and used his foot again. Nothing fancy. He smashed it against the killer's knee. The warrior gasped and his leg buckled. Doug turned and ran. The fellow could still fight, but he was not going to be doing any more running.

Now Doug sprinted. He heard the frustrated cry of the hunters behind him. It spurred him. He dug in hard. His vision blurred through the sweat covering his face. Ahead of him was Tyler's racing figure. The professor had fallen once more into the practiced stride of the long-distance runner.

Doug heard footfalls begin to close on him from behind. One warrior, fleeter than the rest, had pulled ahead of the pack. Doug could hear the warrior's eager panting above his own labored breathing. If he got a hand on Doug, he could delay him long enough for the others to close in. This time Doug did not look back. He put his head down and tore an extra edge of speed from within himself.

The footfalls of the unseen warrior drew no nearer. His breathing took on a ragged tone. Then both sounds began to fade. They receded and were gone. Doug heard angry cries raised from the pack. He prayed that there were no more sprinters among them. He could not afford to slacken his pace and risk it.

Slowly he drew even with Tyler. The professor

looked around in shock and rage. Doug had not intended to pass him. But when Tyler lengthened his stride and pulled ahead, Doug's body responded as if of its own accord. He drew even with Tyler again.

Absurdly, it had become a contest between them. Side by side, with the warriors at their heels, they pitted themselves against each other.

The barrier cliffs at the far end of the valley were definitely closer now. Doug knew without looking that he and Tyler were leaving their pursuers behind. Beside him, Tyler put all of his runner's skill into their bizarre race.

Doug put everything he had into it too. A sense of fleetness began to possess him. His body felt light. Energy pulsed in his veins. His feet seemed barely to touch the ground. He saw Tyler cast a bitter, frustrated glance at him. Tyler sensed what was happening and could do nothing to prevent it. His own wellspring of inner power was depleted.

Doug pulled ahead. He raced on. Tyler, arms pumping convulsively, fell away from the periphery of his vision. Doug surged on in front. Tyler had forced this competition. Now he could live with the results of it.

In front of them Doug saw the wide expanse of a canyon. An inexplicable barrier of heat closed tangibly around him, choking off what breath he had left. He forced his legs to slow their driving strides. He came to a panting, shuddering halt only yards from the canyon's edge. Tyler lurched past him and stumbled to a halt. Doug spun on shaking legs. The warriors were stopping. They were breaking off the pursuit. He and Tyler had passed the second phase of the Proving.

Tyler was bent double, hands on knees, struggling to regain control of his breathing. Doug wanted to do the same. His feeling of fleetness was gone. His chest heaved in painful spasms. He approached the edge of the gorge on feet that had a tendency to stumble. He suspected that the warriors would not give them much time to recover. Soon, they would advance to ensure that he and Tyler entered the third phase of the Proving.

The Abyss of Flames. Looking down, Doug had to shield his eyes from the searing breath of the gorge. He could not see the bottom, only a smoky haze that was shot through with occasional streamers and tongues of flame. Some kind of volcanic rift, he thought, plunging maybe to the fiery core of the earth itself. Here must be the source of the strange cloud that hovered perpetually over the valley. Rising to meet the cooler air above, the humid heat condensed to form the cloud cover.

As he looked, he saw parallel ropes, one some six feet above the other, extending across the seventy-five-yard width of the abyss. The ropes were to be their bridge, he realized with a chill that not even the rising heat could dispel. A test of courage, with death in the flames below the almost certain result of failure.

He looked across the gorge, straining to make out details. The steam and the wavering heat waves distorted his vision. He could not see what awaited them.

It might not matter, anyway, he thought. The flimsy bridge looked grim and treacherous. He wondered how many earlier participants in the Proving had failed to pass this phase and fallen, to be consumed in the inferno.

"We'd better move as soon as possible," he advised Tyler. "They won't let us wait long." His breathing was beginning to return to normal.

Tyler straightened. His face was an impassive mask. He did not acknowledge Doug's statement, but he moved closer to the abyss and studied it intently.

Doug tested the ropes. They appeared securely fastened to a thick stone pillar. Tentatively he gripped the upper rope, then glanced inquiringly around at Tyler. Again Tyler did not directly acknowledge him, but moved to stand closer to the ropes. He opened and closed his hands.

Doug took the upper rope in both hands. It felt almost silky against his palms. He guessed it was made of woven llama hair. It was almost an inch thick and seemed easily capable of supporting his weight. Both of the ropes were stretched nearly taut.

He placed one boot on the lower rope and slid it out over the abyss. The relentless heat made it hard to concentrate. He realized he was gripping the upper rope so tightly that it would surely cause his hands to cramp. He loosened his grip and placed his other foot on the rope. He edged out over the abyss.

Heat buffeted him. His stomach lurched as the lower rope sagged alarmingly beneath his weight. He forced himself to focus on the foot of rope between his fists just in front of his eyes. He wondered despairingly if he could stand the heat. It seemed to press in upon him, sucking moisture from his body.

Slowly, sliding his hands and feet one at a time, he began the crossing. He had to keep closing his eyes against the heat. When he did, his balance spiraled away from him, leaving him clinging desperately. He forced his arms and legs to continue their mechanical movements.

Both ropes surged and swayed sickeningly. He shot a glance back. Tyler had mounted the ropes and was edging forward with determined tenacity. He should have told the professor to wait until he had made the crossing first, Doug berated himself. But the watching warriors might not have allowed it. Doug hoped that Tyler wouldn't try to make another race out of this precarious transit.

A sharp pain began to saw into the muscles beneath Doug's shoulder blades. He realized it was a cramp spawned by the tension clamping his body in a vise. He tried to relax. The pain did not diminish.

The ropes sagged as their combined weights bore them down. Doug imagined his seared skin peeling from him. He felt as though he were being roasted alive. He made himself continue the endless alternating movements of hand and foot, hand and foot.

He guessed—prayed—that he was halfway across now. He risked another glance at Tyler. The other man's face was set in a rigid rictus of bared teeth and squinting eyes. His features were blistered crimson.

The tongue of orange flame that speared up from the fiery depths licked the air only yards in front of Doug. Its upthrust of heat seared him. Instinctively he flung one arm across his eyes. Suspended by only one hand and his feet, he felt himself swing horrifyingly away from the ropes. The awful flame-ridden abyss swept before his red-tinged vision.

The licking tongue of flame sank back into the fiery depths from which it had come. Blindly Doug groped to recapture the rope with his free hand. The abyss clawed at him. His fingers seized the line. He clung to it, eyes pressed tightly shut.

The great pillar of flame had almost consumed him. Another might erupt upward at any moment. It was this thought that made him force his eyelids open. He glanced around for Tyler. Muscles trembling in visible spasms, Tyler hugged the rope. His wild gaze met Doug's.

Doug had no words for him. He couldn't have spoken even if he had. His throat felt burned raw. He unclamped his hand with an effort of will and moved it on down the rope. He slid his boot farther along. He began to move again. The jerk and sway of the ropes told him that Tyler had done likewise. He did not check the professor's progress again. He concentrated on his own.

The rope began to angle slightly upward. They were well past the midpoint. Doug found new strength and speed.

The ledge on the far side was becoming visible. Through the heat-warped haze, Doug could not discern details. It made no difference. Whatever awaited him could not be worse than clinging to this fragile bridge and inching torturously over the mouth of hell.

When he glanced again at the ledge, it was only a few yards distant. Two figures stood waiting impassively well back from the edge. Doug could not afford to look too closely. His cramping hands were wet with sweat. At any moment he might lose his hold on the rope.

With a spine-wrenching contortion he heaved himself the last yard and stepped staggeringly off the rope bridge. He did not let himself collapse. He turned to face the figures awaiting them.

Two warriors confronted him from five yards distant. The foremost one held a pair of war clubs. Without preliminary he tossed one to Doug. One-handed, Doug reached up and caught it. Its unexpected weight made him put a foot back for balance. He was aware of the edge of the abyss close behind his heel.

The club was of solid stone. Its gape-jawed, reptilian head was without the elaborate carving and serrated cutting fangs of the other such weapons that Doug had seen. A training club, then, for use in practice bouts. But a potentially lethal weapon, nonetheless. He gripped the lower end of its haft with both hands, the right inches above the left, in a kendo grip from Japanese fencing. Its bulk felt awkward. The warrior smiled. He lifted his own training club and came in. Maybe this wasn't really better than the abyss.

The warrior struck fast, clearly counting on Doug's weakness from the ordeal to give him the edge. The heavy club slashed over and down at the crown of Doug's skull. Lengthwise, Doug thrust his own club up. Stone smashed against stone as the warrior's club met it and hammered it down against Doug's forehead.

Doug dropped to his knees. His whole skull reverberated like a gong. He glimpsed the warrior swinging his club down and around at his side. Almost blindly, he thrust his weapon out sideways, held horizontally. Again it intercepted the path of the warrior's club. The man grunted at the impact. Doug knew that he couldn't continue to fight for long from his knees. And he didn't know if he could make it to his feet.

He shifted his own club around in an arc, snapping its head against the warrior's unprotected knee. As the leg started to buckle, Doug rammed the head of his club into the descending midriff. The warrior crumpled toward him. Doug caught him with one last stroke to his jaw. He shoved the senseless form to the side as it fell. The warrior's club skipped out into the abyss and was lost.

Doug straightened to his feet with an effort. The remaining warrior stepped forward with one foot. He twirled his club almost as dexterously as Doug had seen Cortozca do back on the plateau. Doug's senses reeled. He was not up to any prolonged exchange of strokes.

He shifted grips on his club and flung it like a spear at the warrior's face.

His shoulder muscles seemed to rip apart with the effort. Shock widened the warrior's eyes. He twitched his club down lengthwise in front of his face. The head of Doug's hurtling club smashed the blocking weapon back full into his countenance. He staggered.

Doug flung himself forward. He swept his right foot around. The side of his boot caught the ankle of the warrior's front foot and carried his leg from under him. Doug hooked his right foot back, not letting it touch down. This time his boot caught the side of the warrior's head with a solid impact. The warrior collapsed atop the two clubs.

Tyler was just stepping free of the bridge. He was trembling with fatigue. He straightened to his full height with an obvious effort. First he looked at the two fallen warriors and then at Doug. One of the warriors, Doug realized, had been meant as Tyler's opponent. If the same thought occurred to Tyler, nothing of it showed on his face.

Doug felt an emptiness that went beyond the physical exhaustion weighting him down. They had passed the Proving and were warriors of Quaztar. Together they had survived. But the bitterness between them was as deep as the abyss over which they had just passed.

Chapter Five

"**H**ere," Ellen said. "Tanztra gave me this and told me to get it to you. Guns are forbidden here, but she suspects that Mixtek has allowed Aguilar and Simon to keep theirs."

Doug took his .45 and its spare magazines from her. They felt good in his hands. He checked them with swift expertise. Satisfied, he handed them back to her. "Do you know how to use it?"

She looked startled. "No."

Doug showed her the essentials. It wasn't much in the way of training in marksmanship and gun safety, but it was the best that circumstances permitted.

They were in a room in the two-story stone house occupied by Tanztra. Even after a night's sleep, Doug's body still ached from the ordeals of the Proving the day before. Ellen had come to him shortly after he had awakened. He had seen little of her following completion of the Proving. He and Tyler had been quickly hustled to adjacent rooms by Dalzar and other warriors loyal to the Queen.

Rising after a night's sleep, he had donned the native clothing left for him. He guessed that he now looked the part of a short-haired, very tan warrior of Quaztar. Ellen, when she appeared, had been clad in a fur leotard and short cape similar to that worn by the Queen. Her long slender legs were bare. Doug had whistled his appreciation. She'd blushed prettily before offering him the gun.

"Have you seen Tyler?" he now asked.

Ellen finished the difficult task of concealing the gun in her clothing. "No," she said. "He's supposed to be next door."

"I know. I checked when I got up, but he wasn't there."

She frowned and looked toward the door as if she might see him there. "I hope he's all right. He was acting so dark and strange yesterday."

Doug resisted the impulse to comfort her with a hug. He remembered the touch of her lips on his. "He probably went exploring," he said to lighten her fears. "He'll be okay." He hoped he was right.

"Tanztra wants to see us," Ellen told him. "There's some kind of ceremony planned for today. It has something to do with the battle up on the plateau yesterday."

"First we need to talk." Doug seated himself on the low stone bed and gestured her to a bench.

"What is it?" she asked intently when she was seated.

"Tyler needs to be in on this, but it can't be helped for now," Doug started. "We have to decide if we plan on trying to escape."

Her eyes widened. "Oh, we mustn't leave!" she exclaimed softly. "Not yet, anyway. Tanztra is in terrible danger. Cortozca and Mixtek would kill her if they thought they could get away with it. They want to seize control of the throne!"

The scenario matched Doug's earlier analysis. "You care about Tanztra, don't you?" he asked.

She nodded quickly. "We sat up and talked most of the night. A lot of the warriors are loyal to her, but she's afraid that Cortozca and the High Priest are plotting to get their hands on enough guns to arm their followers for a takeover. That's why she wanted us on her side. She was desperate when she named me as her adviser. She needs someone who can be her expert on firearms. She really had to agonize over giving you back your gun, since it meant she was violating the law."

"I'll give you a guarantee that Aguilar and Simon are better armed than we are," Doug said with conviction. "And Cortozca told Aguilar up on the plateau that one day he intended to barter for guns."

Ellen shuddered. "Cortozca and Mixtek are awful men. Worse than Aguilar, even."

"I'd call it a draw. Can't Tanztra kick either of them out of office?"

"No. Mixtek's position is hereditary, just like hers. And Cortozca is entitled to be the Queen's Warrior because he is the best fighter among the warriors. None of them can stand against him. All Tanztra can do under the law is refuse to take him as her husband." She made a face at the word and what it implied.

"What happened to the warriors who broke the rules of the Proving in trying to assassinate us?"

"They're in Mixtek's custody. He's assured Tanztra that they will be punished."

"I wouldn't bet on it."

Ellen nodded agreement with his assessment.

Doug drew a deep breath. "So, we'll stay and try to help out."

Her eyes brightened. "Oh, thank you!" Then she sobered. "But *you* could escape. If you stay, it means you'll be risking your life just because of me."

"There are worse reasons." Doug gazed into her eyes. She missed a breath. Doug looked away and went on, "Besides, it's my job to trace Aguilar and find the source of his drugs. I haven't done that. The answer is here, but I don't know what it is yet. I can't leave until I find it. And maybe I can even manage to cut off the flow of the drugs." Briefly he recounted Aguilar's role in the spread of Devil Dust through the drug world.

"Tyler will want to stay too," she said with certainty. "He'll see this as one great field trip."

Doug couldn't read the emotions in her tone. He

recalled the brooding bitterness over their rivalry he had sensed in Tyler. But he didn't mention it to Ellen.

She slapped her hands down on her knees. "We have to go. I told Tanztra I'd bring you right back."

"There's one last thing." Doug rose. Her eyes questioned him as he moved to stand over her. Gently he took her shoulders and drew her to her feet. He saw her eyes widen slightly before he kissed her. Her response was gentle and yearning.

He held her in his arms when they drew apart. "I've been wanting to do that properly." His voice was hoarse.

"I've been wanting you to," she whispered, and then wriggled from his grasp. "Come on." She caught his hand.

Tanztra was pacing like a lioness when they entered her spacious chambers. Llama rugs and the skins of other, unidentifiable animals adorned the floor and couches in barbaric luxury.

Tanztra exhaled sharply as she saw them. "You're here," she said. "I was becoming worried." Her eyes lingered on Doug. "You have rested? You did well in the Proving," she went on before he could answer. "Where is your companion?"

Ellen explained Tyler's strange absence. Doug studied the Queen. She was no longer a young girl, but her elegant beauty would have graced the most cosmopolitan of settings.

She called out briskly when Ellen had finished. A warrior appeared, and Tanztra issued terse orders to locate Tyler. The warrior disappeared. She turned back to her guests.

"We do not have much time," she said to Doug. "There is to be a ceremony honoring the God of the Dark Waters. As new warriors, you and your companion are required to attend. I want you both near me and Ellen as part of my retinue."

"Expecting trouble?" Doug asked.

As Tanztra shook her head, her blond hair swirled about her bare shoulders. "I don't think that Mixtek and Cortozca would try anything during the ceremony, but the ceremony itself is unpredictable. There will be an . . . offering made to the god." She broke off and drew her finger from her lower lip down the length of her neck in her characteristic reflective gesture. Doug sensed that there was something she wanted to add to what she had already said. But she shook her head in vexation and remained silent.

"How did your people come to worship this God of the Dark Waters?" he probed. He recalled Tyler's assertion that the mysterious deity wasn't one of the traditional gods once worshiped in this region.

"The god was not always with us." Tanztra began a slow prowl of the room as she spoke. Doug noted the stone dagger at her waist. "Many lifetimes ago, we defended our land against the invaders. At that time our city occupied not only the Great Cavern but spread across the mountains. Gradually, as the newcomers—Ellen says you call them Incas—grew stronger and pressed in upon us, we were forced to retreat from the rest of our city and into the Cavern, where they could not assault us without great losses. Eventually they left us alone, although they would not allow us to emerge from the valley. They razed our city on the mountains until only rubble remained. We knew then that our gods had deserted us. We sought new ones."

As she paused, her pale eyes seemed to be staring into that lost past of warring tribes and vanished cities. A shudder passed over her. "Then the God of the Dark Waters came," she said. "In a single night the mountains moved and shook. Our cavern city collapsed around us. Many were killed. A great chasm opened in the cavern floor, and when morning came, the cavern had been flooded by waters from deep in the earth, as you see it now."

Doug tried to envision the cataclysmic upheaval that had created the vast sunless sea and toppled the subterranean city. "How did the god come?" he asked softly.

"He appeared in the waters of the lake." Tanztra's eyes grew wide and fearful. "A new temple and an altar were established to the God of the Dark Waters. They still stand on the shore of the lake. The temple is where you were first brought before us. A high priest was named, and the priests of our old gods were slain. The new high priest declared that we had angered the god and that we were not to rebuild our cavern city. Instead, as penance, we were to build a humble city outside the cavern and dwell there." Her voice grew lower. "Over the lifetimes, our numbers have shrunk. We are no longer mighty. Our laws forbid us from leaving the valley to have contact with interlopers."

"You know that Cortozca was trading with Aguilar outside the valley." Doug had made it a statement.

Tanztra gave a troubled nod. "I permitted it when he and Mixtek insisted. It is contrary to our ancient laws, but it was Mixtek's ancestor, the first high priest, who declared the laws. I do not know how Cortozca made contact with Aguilar. We needed the healing kits that he was able to provide for us. Many of our children are born sickly now. They are weak and often succumb to disease. Their bodies and spirits are frail."

Generations of inbreeding and isolation under the dominion of a harsh religion were finally taking their inevitable toll on this race, Doug realized. "What's traded for the kits?" he asked.

"The Fire Lichen."

"What's that?"

"You saw it in the Cavern. It provides the light. It appeared shortly after the coming of the god. The first high priest discovered its qualities."

Doug felt his teeth grind together. The lichen was probably some mutant vegetation spawned in the black depths of the cave and then nurtured in the unique environment created by the ancient earthquake. "What are its qualities?" he asked.

Something in his voice made Tanztra's gaze grow wary. "When it is ground to a powder and swallowed or breathed, it lifts the emotions. Too much can make the user like a maddened beast and give him the strength of many."

"It can also kill," Doug said tightly. He was barely aware of Ellen's hand on his arm.

"I know," Tanztra whispered. "Only the High Priest is permitted to use it without restriction."

Doug recalled the subdued yellow fire in Mixtek's eyes. He should have realized it earlier. The High Priest was addicted to Devil Dust.

"And the Queen's Warrior, when going into battle, is permitted to use it freely," Tanztra added.

The idea of Cortozca's prowess heightened by Devil Dust was chilling. He now knew the source of the drug, Doug mused, and it was no wonder that Aguilar was the only supplier to the outside world. "The dust of the Fire Lichen has done great harm in my land," he said, trying to keep his voice even.

Tanztra bowed her head. Her long hair fell forward around her face like a pale shroud. "I was afraid of that," she confessed softly. "But the healing kits were useful, and my authority is already threatened by Cortozca and Mixtek. I would not force a confrontation by opposing them on this matter. I feared the outcome if I did. Never in our history have the High Priest and the Queen's Warrior opposed a Queen so openly. Perhaps I have erred by allowing them to gain so much power." She drew her finger down her throat. "Maybe, if I had taken Cortozca as my husband when he demanded it, I could have prevented this, but knowing him as I do, I couldn't marry him. I couldn't. . . ."

Her aloofness had dissolved beneath the burdens of her leadership. Ellen went to her.

"Forget it," Doug said. "Accepting him as your husband would've been wrong, and it wouldn't have helped. Cortozca and Mixtek are too corrupt to ever be satisfied. You would've just made things worse."

Tanztra composed herself with an obvious effort. The look she flashed Doug was unreadable, but it touched something inside him.

"We must go to the ceremony," she said with resolution. An apprehension of disaster seemed to brush across her face. She shook her head. "Come."

An escort of warriors joined them outside the house. Dalzar was their leader. He fell in beside Doug as they headed toward the gigantic mouth of the cavern.

"You fought well in the Proving," Dalzar said with sincerity.

"I couldn't have done so without your warnings," Doug told him.

Dalzar shook his head. "No, you would have passed the Proving even had I not given you warning. You are a born warrior." His glance moved briefly to Tanztra's regal figure in front of them. "I am glad you are one of us."

Doug nodded thoughtfully. They were joined by

two warriors with Tyler at the cavern mouth. The professor still wore his khaki outfit, which was ragged now. The miniature computer and his walkie-talkie were sheathed on his belt. Ellen ran to him. Doug could not hear their words. Ellen stepped quickly back as if stung. Tyler gazed blackly at Doug over her head. She turned away from him. Her face was troubled. Doug had no chance to ask what had happened before they were moving into the cavern.

A good part of the populace was already present. They lined the shores of the lake in silent, somehow fearful groupings. The dark waters swirled sluggishly in the eerie light of the Fire Lichen.

An exterior stairway led to the roof of the stone temple. From that vantage point they could see a stately procession approaching the adjacent altar. Mixtek paced in the lead. He carried a yard-long conical object in outstretched palms with reverence. Even from a distance Doug could see the golden glare of his eyes. Mixtek was flying on Devil Dust.

A little behind him strode Cortozca like some alabaster colossus given breath and animation. Other warriors were behind them. In their midst was a somnambulistic figure. Doug squinted in the poor light and recognized the desperado he had seen kicking the fallen warrior during the abortive ambush on the plateau. This must be the prisoner Ellen had seen from their cell.

The captive moved like a zombie in a horror movie. He appeared oblivious to his surroundings.

His face was blank. "What's wrong with him?" Doug asked Tanztra.

"He has been given a special dilution of the Fire Lichen. It prepares him for what is to come." Again the troubled spirit touched her features.

She fell silent.

"Who is he?"

"He is a follower of El Demonio, an interloper who has tried to bring his men into our valley in the past. They have a camp in the mountains. They raid and pillage throughout this area. They have long been enemies of our people."

Some kind of bandit chieftain and his attendant rabble, Doug supposed. He remembered the ugly savagery of the trio in El Dolor and the attackers on the plateau. He could feel little sympathy for the captive, but the hairs on his neck bristled as the man was led atop the high altar.

He could feel Ellen's tension where she stood on his other side. The passive captive was bound spread-eagled between the stone pillars surmounting the altar. Ellen's fingers interlaced with Doug's and gripped tightly.

The warriors filed down from the altar. Cortozca was last. He turned toward the dark, heaving waters of the sea and lifted his ornate war club in an odd kind of challenging salute. He followed his warriors. Mixtek was alone on the altar with the captive.

For a moment the priest stood motionless, a figure of dark and evil menace. The watching crowd began to utter a low, wordless paean. Threads of grief and fear were woven through the unnerving sound. The crowd seemed to shift like the surface of the sea.

Solemnly Mixtek lifted the tapering cylinder. He placed the small end to his lips. Doug realized it was some kind of horn. The note that emerged was a high, trembling wail. It swelled and filled the cavern. Doug wanted to cover his ears. Mixtek lowered the horn at last. The tones of the strange note lingered chillingly, obscuring the dying chant of the crowd.

Doug's eyes were drawn to the sunless sea. Was it his imagination or did there seem to be a new motion swirling out there on its black surface? Again Mixtek lifted the horn, and the eerie note wailed across the cavern. As he lowered the horn, he stared intently over the lake. The paean of the crowd fell away into trembling silence. Mixtek turned, strode to the stairway, and descended the altar. Doug detected an urgency to his step.

As Ellen gasped, Doug looked at the lake. He had a peripheral image of Tanztra's rigid features. Her pale hair seemed to glow in the reflected phosphorescence. "I tried to stop this," she said with sudden intensity. "Please remember that. *I tried to stop it!*"

Out on the sea, the waters swirled and danced. Something huge heaved up from the surface and rushed toward the shore. Twin rolls of water swept across the lake like the legs of a widening V. The submerged object's passage slowed as it neared shore. The water churned. A dark shape broke the surface.

Two red flames glinted from it. Someone in the crowd screamed. Up from the water arose an evil reptilian head atop a pale sinuous column of flesh. Snakelike, it swayed forty feet above the water. Behind it, Doug glimpsed the broad rounded surface of its back.

The creature moved shoreward, its neck tilted forward. The fanged jaws opened and hissed. At that moment Doug saw the inspiration for the tattoos of Mixtek's warriors and the deadly carved heads of the war clubs. The God of the Dark Waters had come in answer to the High Priest's ritual summons. It heaved itself up on the shore on seallike flippers. Its oval body and short, tapering tail added another forty feet to its length. With surprising agility it lurched toward the altar.

"A plesiosaur!" Ellen cried.

"I thought they were extinct," Doug said.

Ellen shook her head emphatically. She was all but breathless with excitement. "There have been sightings from all over the world. Take Loch Ness, for example. And in 1977 some Japanese fishermen caught and photographed a plesiosaur in their nets before throwing its carcass back into the sea."

Whatever the accuracy of the reports, there was no denying the reality of the great creature before them. Its hiss blasted forth like air being released from a giant gas balloon. The sound swelled into a wailing roar that shuddered back and forth between the walls of the huge cavern. It flippered its way forward. Water streamed down from its whitish bulk. Like the human inhabitants of the valley, the beast seemed to have lost much of the pigmentation of its skin. Its eyes gleamed like evil rubies in its gargoyle skull.

Tanztra's fingers dug painfully into Doug's arm. With belated horror Doug realized the purpose of the ceremony and the function of the bandit suspended helpless on the altar. His shout of protest was lost in the monster's second reverberating roar. Doug detected an awful, ravening hunger in the sound.

The monster's bulk dwarfed the altar. Its fanged head hovered above the captive. For a moment it hesitated. Then the horrible head darted down with appalling speed. Like a toy, the bandit was plucked effortlessly from his bindings. Doug stared in horror. The desperado had vanished. He had uttered no sound when the monster's jaws had closed about him. In his drugged state he had apparently felt nothing.

The monster's maw gaped. The altar stood empty. The beast backed away. Its head swiveled about on the end of its long neck. It hissed in the direction of the watching crowd.

Another sound arose, and Doug saw Mixtek again wielding the ceremonial horn. Higher and shriller than before the note sounded. The plesiosaur snapped like a dog at a circling wasp. The long neck writhed. Its four flippers slapped at the stone shore as it lurched into an awkward turn. Mixtek continued to blow on the horn.

The beast splashed back into the water. One last time its roar bounced echoes through the height and breadth of the cavern. And then its neck arched and its head disappeared beneath the water. In moments, the great bulk of its body also slid from sight. The water swirled into uneasy stillness in its wake.

Ellen's mouth was strained wide in an eerie, silent scream. Tanztra buried her face against Doug's shoulder and clung to his arm with both hands. "I tried." Her voice was muffled. "I couldn't stop it from happening!" She drew herself erect.

Mixtek had appeared once more on the altar. Beside him towered the sculpted figure of Cortozca. "Hear me!" The High Priest's words penetrated dimly the numb horror overlying Doug's mind.

The High Priest lifted his arms. "The God of the Dark Waters has accepted our offering. Yesterday, the interlopers of El Demonio attacked our warriors. For that outrage, the god has been appeased. But their actions cannot go unavenged. The god's honor must be restored!"

"Warriors of Quaztar!" Cortozca called out on an apparent cue. "I command a Congregation of Warriors immediately! Gather now in the training field. I summon you to your duty as warriors! We will restore the honor of the god!"

Doug sensed dark political maneuverings behind the announcements. He had no time for them. Harsh words grated unspoken behind his teeth. Tanztra's frantic pleading look choked them off. He let the Queen usher him and Ellen through a roof doorway into the chamber below.

"Tanztra! How could you let that happen?" Ellen's cry of betrayal and outrage forestalled his own bitter words.

Tanztra pressed her face into her hands. "I cannot prevent it!" she cried in a muffled sob. "The laws have always sanctioned such offerings to the god. I know it is wrong. I know it—"

"That thing's not God!" Doug broke in angrily. "It's not even *a* god! It's just an animal trapped in that lake and conditioned to obey the sounds of that horn."

Tanztra nodded mutely. Her anguish was evident. "I have sought to stop the offerings, but the ancient laws permit them. At times, they even require them. My own power depends on the laws. I must choose how and when I oppose them or I lose my authority. Don't you see?"

Doug's outrage dimmed. He looked helplessly at Ellen. Compassion warred with the fading horror on her face. She went tenderly to Tanztra and hugged her like a sister.

Doug drew a deep, shuddering breath. He could not believe that the horror of those moments in the cavern would ever leave him completely. But Tanztra could not be held wholly to blame.

He did not know how the plesiosaur might have

survived. Perhaps Ellen was correct, and others of its species were extant in remote areas of the globe. Released from some unimaginable subterranean vault by the ancient earthquake, the creature must have found other marine life in the lake to sustain it. Maybe this was not even the same animal that had originally emerged. It was possible that, like some other animals known to science, the plesiosaur was androgynous, able to reproduce without a mate. Successive generations might have inhabited the lake over the centuries.

"What is this Congregation of the Warriors that Cortozca has called?" he asked Tanztra.

"The Queen's Warrior calls a Congregation only before leading the warriors into battle."

"Against El Demonio?"

"It must be. Cortozca does not consult me in such matters." She hesitated. "Whatever it is, either you or Tyler must accompany the war march."

Doug looked at Ellen. She bit her lower lip. Doug realized he had lost track of Tyler during the hellish ceremony.

"I'll go," he said flatly. He did not relish the idea of leaving Ellen and marching off to some distant battlefield, but to let Tyler go unprotected into combat would be to commit him to death. He turned away so that he wouldn't see Ellen's troubled eyes.

Chapter Six

Doug turned his training club and parried Dalzar's strike. The heavy weapons crashed together. Doug was becoming familiar with the weight of his weapon. It was not so different from Japanese fencing with an extremely heavy sword. He parried again. The sounds of their mock combat joined the clatter of the other warriors training on the field outside the village.

Dalzar stepped back and grinned. "You have a true skill, my brother," he said.

Doug's arms and shoulders ached. The club was much heavier than any of the other martial-arts weapons with which he had trained.

There were almost two hundred warriors practicing their skills in the field, he estimated. After the ceremony in the cavern, Cortozca had addressed the warriors gathered on the field. As expected, he had announced a raid on the camp of El Demonio the following morning. The news had been greeted with eagerness by the warriors. They were tired of raids by El Demonio when they ventured out of the valley.

Cortozca had directed them to spend the afternoon honing their skills and their weapons. Doug had caught sight of the Queen's Warrior prowling the training field. He had not seen Tyler since the ceremony.

Doug hefted his club for another set-to with Dalzar. The more experienced he was with the weapon, the higher the odds of his survival tomorrow. He had not forgotten the firearms of the desperadoes.

"You have learned our ways quickly, interloper," a deep voice jeered.

Doug turned to see Cortozca observing him from a few yards away. A group of tattooed warriors were clustered at his back. Doug kept his club lifted to a guard position.

"I'm pleased the Queen's Warrior is satisfied with my progress." His voice carried the edge of one of the stone daggers.

Cortozca turned and spat. "You were in luck to pass the Proving," he said contemptuously. "But it is reported that you fought well even without a weapon, using only your empty hands."

"I had no other weapons," Doug reminded him drily. He studied Cortozca. Seen this close, the Queen's Warrior was truly awesome.

"I have no weapons." Cortozca lifted his muscular arms. "Do you think you could beat me with your empty hands?"

"I don't know," Doug answered evenly.

Cortozca's thick lips lifted in a sneer that was almost a snarl. "Put down your club and we shall see."

Slowly Doug lowered the club. He was vaguely conscious of Dalzar's stricken expression. He didn't know if there was any way of avoiding this match. He did know that he didn't want to avoid it.

As the warriors behind Cortozca backed clear, Doug passed his club to Dalzar. He shrugged off the warrior's protesting hand. Cortozca stepped forward. He shifted shoulders and arms in a supple fashion that flexed and relaxed the rippling muscles of his torso.

Doug assessed his opponent. Cortozca was undoubtedly bigger and stronger and possibly faster than he. He would be an expert in the unarmed fighting style of Quaztar. Doug had seen the style practiced, both during the Proving and on the training field. He guessed that it must be largely a static form, shielded from any contact with other fighting styles by the remoteness of the valley. But it could still be deadly. He shifted his left side toward Cortozca and raised his half-open hands.

Cortozca emitted an explosive grunt. He side-hopped in. His torso leaned far to the side to counterbalance the thick leg he drove at Doug in a stamping side kick. The Queen's Warrior plainly wanted this contest ended fast, and his kick had the power to do it. Doug pivoted to the outside, behind Cortozca. He sensed the raw force behind the kick as Cortozca's leg thrust past him. He snapped the ball of his foot hard against Cortozca's exposed kidney. Cortozca's massive body shivered with the impact.

He spun toward Doug in the next instant. The edges of both open hands came slashing around with his turn. Cortozca's speed was little, if any, short of Doug's own. As Doug leaned back, the tips of Cortozca's fingers grazed his chest. They felt like iron. Doug shifted his torso forward into the corkscrewing straight-arm blow that he rammed solidly to Cortozca's skull.

Again Cortozca's body shuddered. Doug hoped he would drop. It had been a good blow. But Cortozca stayed on his feet and swung around. Doug had expected the stamping kicks and spinning edge of the hand techniques. Now Cortozca used a new tactic. The stiffened fingers of both his hands stabbed simultaneously at Doug's face like spears.

Desperately Doug ducked. He felt the hard fingers scrape across the top of his head. He had time for a single blow to Cortozca's midriff. It was like punching stone. He glimpsed the slashing movements of Cortozca's hands overhead. He tried to dodge back and was too slow. Again Cortozca had struck with both hands simultaneously. The edge of one palm smashed down to the side of Doug's neck. The other, palm up, sliced against his ribs.

It was like being hit by electric cattle prods. Doug convulsed and fell to one knee. Bolts of pain ripped through him. Dimly he saw the massive columns of

Cortozca's legs in front of him. He sensed Cortozca towering overhead, hand uplifting for another blow. He would never survive it.

Doug twisted his shoulders and wrapped his right arm around Cortozca's right leg. He hugged it to him and got both feet under him, throwing his shoulders up into Cortozca's midriff. He heard Cortozca grunt. His groping left hand sank into the muscles of Cortozca's chest. He straightened and heaved up and over. Cortozca's giant form flipped over him. The Queen's Warrior crashed to the field flat on his back. Doug reeled from the effort of throwing the bigger man. His temples pounded. He was vaguely aware that their contest had drawn a growing crowd of spectators.

Cortozca whirled up onto his feet with a warrior's reflexes. He seemed stunned, more from shock than from the physical damage of the fall. Doug understood suddenly that the unarmed combat techniques of Quaztar didn't include throws and grappling techniques such as the one he had used.

Elation forced back the red tides of pain surging within him. He tried to mask his sudden satisfaction. Shakily he lifted his hands. Rage replaced the bemusement in Cortozca's eyes. He came gliding in and stabbed his stiffened right fingers at Doug's throat.

Doug tilted his body to the outside, and then parried across his chest with the heel of his left palm. He swung his right leg past Cortozca and behind the warrior's right leg on the outside. Like a swinging fence post, his stiffened right arm swept around against Cortozca's massive chest. In the same instant he swung his right leg back. His right calf came hard against that of Cortozca. His swinging arm levered the warrior back and over that leg. Again Cortozca hit the ground.

Even the Queen's Warrior could not sustain many such impacts without the benefit of knowing how to break his falls. Doug's snapping kick jerked his head to one side as he scrambled awkwardly to regain his feet. Doug moved clear. Cortozca roared in fury. All vestige of training sloughed from him. He lunged with rending hands for Doug's throat.

Doug whirled with the attack. He took Cortozca's lunging weight on his hip and back and flipped him up over his doubled form. He felt the ground vibrate beneath his feet at the warrior's impact. Cortozca flailed weakly. Doug flung himself down atop him. His plunging knee rammed full into Cortozca's solar plexus. The Queen's Warrior jackknifed forward. Three times the edge of Doug's fist pounded against his rock-hard temple. Cortozca's great body subsided.

Doug pushed himself up and away from the prostrate form. He was afraid that Cortozca might revive to envelop him in those massive arms. Then Dalzar came to his side and steadied him. There was a look of awe in the warrior's face. A murmur rippled through the spectators.

Cortozca was already beginning to stir. Doug

could hardly believe it. Two tattooed warriors rushed forward to assist him. His flailing arms drove them back. Half doubled in pain, Cortozca rose unsteadily to his feet. He straightened to his full height. Doug shifted clear of Dalzar.

Cortozca said, "You would not have fared so well had we fought with war clubs, as true warriors fight. Perhaps someday we shall."

"Maybe when you've recovered from this time," Doug replied. He turned and walked quickly away, trying to keep his legs steady. Dalzar accompanied him. The ranks of warriors parted before them.

Exhaustion weighted Doug's steps. He needed to rest. The fight with Cortozca had been grueling. He was not misleading himself. In unarmed combat, his training in a variety of styles and forms had given him an edge on Cortozca. With war clubs, it might well be different. He did not favor his chances if he ever had to face Cortozca on the other man's terms.

The image of the great prehistoric beast rising from the murky water to claim his helpless victim haunted Ellen. She tossed fitfully on the fur-covered couch. She tried, with scientific dispassion, to dispel the images. She couldn't. At last she sat up in defeat.

She was alone in her private chamber, adjacent to Tanztra's. The Queen was engaged in her administrative duties. Seeing Ellen's exhaustion, she had ordered her to rest. Ellen had been only too glad to comply. The emotional and physical strains of the past few hours, climaxing in the horrible ceremony, had drained her strength.

Had all this happened in only two days? Had she really been in a gunfight, discovered a lost civilization, found a dear friend, and fallen in love? It seemed impossible. But there was no denying it, especially the fact that she had fallen in love with a handsome, daring undercover drug enforcement agent.

Where was Doug? she wondered. Was he still at the Congregation of Warriors, whatever that might entail? A pang of worry troubled her as she recalled the obvious enmity that the Queen's Warrior, Cortozca, held for Doug. Could even Doug hope to have a chance against an opponent as fearsome as Cortozca?

And where was Dick? Until yesterday, he had been the most important man in her life. She had lost track of him too. Lost track of him in more ways than one, she mused sadly.

She had sensed deep changes taking place darkly within him. He was no longer the challenging and admirable mentor who had guided her skillfully through the torturous ways of academia, drawing forth talents she had never dreamed she possessed. He was changing. Had changed. He was someone else now, and she didn't like it. But she was unable to prevent or even understand the change.

Despondently, she lay back on the soft furs, conscious of the hard stone beneath. She gazed up at the stone ceiling. Even if she couldn't sleep, it felt good just to relax.

She should go to Tanztra, who might have need of her. There was a curious satisfaction in being near Tanztra. Ellen had been an only child. She had never known the intimate bonds that can form between sisters. She sensed such a bonding now between her and Tanztra. She savored it.

And the demands of her scholarly life, including the fascinating presence of Dickinson Tyler, had left her little time for any other kinds of relationships. She found herself savoring the forging of other bonds as well. The image of Doug hovered in her mind. What would he look like with his hair cut and wearing a nice suit when he wasn't playing the dangerous role of a drug dealer? Had she read in his eyes the same emotions that she knew were growing inside herself?

Resolutely she rose from the couch. *Enough lying around,* she told herself. She would find Tanztra. Perhaps the queen would have word of Doug. And Dick.

As she freshened up, she remembered Doug's appreciative whistle when he had first seen her that morning. It would be fun to dress to please him, she mused.

Finished, she hurried to the door. She recoiled as it opened by itself.

"My lady," Aguilar said with slithery politeness. Behind the drug lord lurked Simon, his gunman.

"What do you want?" Ellen demanded. She did

not know how the sleazy pair had gained access to the Queen's quarters. She resisted the impulse to call for help.

"A few words with you," Aguilar answered her in oily tones. He edged forward as if to force her to retreat into her room. She stood her ground. Under no circumstances was she going to permit herself to be alone in a closed room with this pair. She yearned for Doug's commanding presence.

"I'm in a hurry," she began defensively. It was a poor start, she realized. After all, she was Maiden Adviser to the Queen and not without standing and authority. "Speak and speak quickly!" she snapped. That was better.

Aguilar blinked at her assertiveness. "We must discuss a few matters," he tried again.

"You and I have nothing to discuss!" What did the man want? While she would not retreat, she could not summon the fortitude to push past them. The idea of physical contact with them was revolting. A stench radiated from Aguilar. She did not know if it was him or his faded, multicolored poncho.

She saw that Simon had some kind of stubby gun slung openly over his shoulder. It was what Doug would call an assault gun. The .45 he had given her lay out of reach on a stone table where she had placed it when dressing. It was uncomfortable to carry. She vowed never to be without it again.

"Things will change here soon," Aguilar stated. He tilted his head slowly from side to side as he spoke. "Now the Queen protects you, but that may not always be. There are others here who would offer you sanctuary and—pleasures."

"You, for instance?" she sneered.

Aguilar bared fangs. There was no other description for it. "You are mine, *niña,*" he declared. "Now or later, it does not matter to me, except that later, it will not be so easy for you as it would be if you now accept what I offer."

"Get out of here!" she cried.

"You are foolish, *niña.*" Aguilar's eyes slid up and down her body. "Perhaps I shall make your choice for you now." He lifted one hand from beneath the poncho. Ellen glimpsed Simon's leering grin. She would turn and try for the .45, her mind flashed desperately. She knew she would not make it.

"Why are you here?" a stern voice demanded unexpectedly.

Ellen's knees went weak with relief as she saw the powerful figure of Dalzar looming in the corridor. *Thank you, God!*

Aguilar spun around as if yanked. Simon's hand flew reflexively to his stubby gun. Dalzar had approached with feline stealth. He leaned slightly forward on the balls of his feet. His heavy war club was half raised. Ellen understood he was in a subtle combat posture. He was close enough to do damage with his club in the same interval it would take Simon to bring his gun to bear.

The two drug dealers realized it too. A sideward

flick of Aguilar's eyes made Simon's hand slip away from the gun.

"We have business with the Maiden Adviser," Aguilar said swiftly.

"They have no business with me!" Ellen denied angrily. "They are intruders here!"

"Go!" Dalzar's tone said that he understood well what he had interrupted. "Even the Counsel of the High Priest is no more than a man when a war club is wielded against him. His flesh will bleed and his bones will break." He hefted his weapon ominously.

"I will wait, *niña,*" Aguilar murmured, and started away. Simon retreated with him.

Hard flames flickered in Dalzar's eyes as he watched them go. "Leave the Queen's manor, or it will not go well with you."

Ellen wanted to hug him. She stiffened her knees as he turned his concerned gaze on her. "Are you all right?" he asked solicitously.

She nodded mutely.

"I returned early with Doug from the Congregation. He asked me to check on your safety while he rested."

"Is he all right?" Ellen asked. "Can you take me to him?"

Dalzar nodded. "He will wish to know what has happened here. He won a great victory against the Queen's Warrior on the training field."

"You won one here," Ellen assured him gratefully.

Chapter Seven

The lair of El Demonio was a motley collection of shacks and huts in a stony defile of the mountains. A couple of dilapidated vehicles indicated a contact with the outer world. Crouched in concealment with other warriors in the rocky crags overhead, Doug grimaced in disgust at the foul odors drifting up from the encampment.

He could see a number of shabby men and women moving about the structure in the relative warmth of the late afternoon. Most of the men carried firearms. Though the weapons were not sophisticated, they would still give the bandits an edge against attackers armed with stone clubs.

Doug glanced to where Cortozca surveyed the scene. The hundred warriors in the war party had marched through the day under Cortozca's leadership to reach their current vantage point. They had eaten jerked meat on the march. The route had taken them over and around mountain peaks and along nearly invisible paths scarring the faces of sheer cliffs.

Doug had tense memories of panoramic displays of breathtaking mountain scenery viewed precariously from muscle-straining perches among barren crags. They had passed deep pockets of snow in perpetual shadow. Far overhead, Doug had seen great Andean condors wheeling in slow, endless circles.

They would wait until dark to attack, Cortozca had declared. The desperadoes were estimated to be about seventy-five in number. Given their firearms, a night assault was the wisest strategy, Doug admitted.

The warrior beside Doug tensed. "El Demonio," he whispered in near-fearful tones.

Doug looked at the camp. He saw an enormous mestizo emerging from the largest shack. Muscles and fat strained at his filthy clothing. A battered sombrero was perched atop a head of greasy shoulder-length hair.

Arrogantly, El Demonio strutted about his tiny empire. Most of his followers shrank away from him. One slovenly woman, bolder than the rest, ventured near. She spoke to the bandit leader. Her manner was supplicatory. Without warning, El Demonio's hand lashed out. There was speed as well as strength in the massive arm. The woman was knocked off her feet. El Demonio tried to stomp on her. She scrambled away frantically. El Demonio's brutal laughter reached the watchers clearly.

The Demon had earned his name, Doug reflected grimly.

He guessed that this unsavory crew subsisted on raids on villages, herdsmen, and isolated homesteads, and then retreated here to their remote enclave until their next assault. Doug tightened his grip on his club. He had no qualms about participating in the attack.

Cortozca signaled with his hands. The warriors were to surround the camp and wait in concealment until the deep of night before launching their assault. Groups of them began to fade away into the rocky wilderness. Doug recalled the eerie stealth with which the warriors had captured him and Ellen and Tyler. He was seeing it demonstrated again. He eased away from where he crouched.

Darkness seemed to drop out of the sky to cloak the barren peaks. For a moment they were gray shadows. Then they were no more than looming black shapes against the night. Hard diamond stars flickered overhead.

Doug studied the profiles of the six warriors with whom he waited. None of them bore the plesiosaur tattoo of Mixtek's minions. On the march they had been friendly to Doug and respectful of his victory over Cortozca. He felt a growing kinship with them. He missed the competent presence of Dalzar, however. The warrior had stayed behind to coordinate the protection of Tanztra and Ellen.

When the moon looked down on them from directly overhead, the warriors stirred. Doug sensed the poised, electrical charge that crackled from men about to go into combat. No training weapon this time. The stone head of his club snarled silently at him.

Doug moved with the warriors into the darkness. An infernal glow glared from the defile where the squalid encampment was located. Reaching the edge, Doug saw that a large central bonfire was slowly dying. Some of the bandits sprawled asleep or unconscious on the ground. Shadows crept about their still forms. It took Doug a moment to realize that the shadows were enormous rats, foraging openly amidst the refuse of the camp. He drew a slow breath to quell his nausea before moving forward. The other warriors followed.

They separated as they slipped down toward the camp. Attacking in groups would make them more vulnerable to gunfire. In moments, the pale skin of his companions was lost in the darkness. All around the encampment, Doug pictured other warriors descending upon their unsuspecting victims.

He glimpsed a powerful figure off to his right. For just an instant, moonlight caught the handsome features of Cortozca. Doug's blood chilled. The eyes of the Queen's Warrior glowed with a hellish yellow fire. Devil Dust. As was his irrevocable right, Cortozca had used the drug in preparation for battle.

For a moment, Doug felt those flaming eyes burn through him. Then Cortozca seemed to dematerialize into the ether. In a flicker he was gone. Doug shivered and went on.

He dropped low to the ground as he neared the floor of the defile. He knew that there would be guards. It had been impossible to pinpoint them in the dark. He used the rocks for cover. Metal clicked against stone ahead, and he froze.

Cautiously he peered through the night. A slouching figure prowled casually at the edge of the camp. Doug laid his club gently aside. He drew the stone dagger at his waist and eased forward.

The guard was almost sleepwalking. He stumbled once, and Doug took him down with cold, detached efficiency. He let the body slump. The hilt of the dagger was tight in his fist. There would be time later for the sickness and horror at what he had done. He could not afford it now.

Swiftly he knelt to examine his victim. His hand brushed familiar metallic lines. He worked the object clear of its owner. It was a Chinese version of the Russian AK-47 assault rifle, and he was able to identify it by feel as much as by sight. The folding stock and bayonet were both collapsed.

Doug gripped the weapon thoughtfully. There were better versions of the gun, but this was still a formidable piece, far superior to anything he had expected to find here, and his possession of it would give him a devastating advantage in what was to come. But it would also demonstrate to Cortozca just how effective a simple assault weapon could be in combat. And Cortozca would undoubtedly demand possession of it after the battle.

Doug carried it with him as he went back to retrieve his club. He left the rifle concealed there in the rocks. The less Cortozca knew of such weapons, the better.

An agonized scream ripped out of the darkness on the far side of the camp. And then a shotgun roared. Doug snarled under his breath. One of the warriors had not made his kill a clean one.

Doug ran forward into the camp. He saw other warriors rushing in from the darkness and heard excited, questioning shouts from the awakening bandits. A giant rat ran across his foot. Human figures sprang into view from shacks and huts. Decadent or not, the desperadoes were quick in reacting to an attack on their camp.

Doug skidded to a halt in front of a tilting shack as a bearded man erupted from within. The bandit held an ancient carbine in a clumsy port position. Another figure loomed behind him.

The foremost bandit growled like a beast as he tried to swing the carbine down into line. Doug put his shoulders into a downward slanting cut from right to left. He felt the stone teeth of his club bite into flesh at the man's neck. The bandit yelled and reeled sideward and away.

Doug had an instant's view of the leveled barrels of the sawed-off shotgun held by the second desperado. His wrists popped and pain stabbed up his arms as he flipped the heavy club over, down, and around. Its jawed head clanged against the barrels of the stubby weapon and batted it wide as twin explosions roared from it. Doug felt the shock and heat graze his side like a kick. He let the club continue on its course up and around, twisting his wrists as he did so. Once more the stone fangs slashed down from right to left. The desperado's knees buckled lifelessly.

A thunderbolt cracked past Doug's head. He spun around from his falling victim. Four yards away another bandit was awkwardly thumbing back the hammer of his old revolver for a second shot. Doug shifted his club in front of his chest as the revolver roared. The club shivered in his hands. The ricochet whined past his ear. He snatched out his dagger and flung it in a circular sweep. He no more than glimpsed its hurtling flight before it drove into its target. The desperado died with shock still on his face.

Doug ran to recover the dagger. Crouched over his victim, he took an instant to survey the camp. Dark figures ran and fought and died in the shifting light and shadows of the fading bonfire.

He saw two warriors flayed in a ripping fusillade of gunfire from a quartet of bandits. The four desperadoes had closed ranks and were covering one another with the skill of experienced combat veterans. Doug knew the danger in their professional tactics. Working together, the quartet could turn the tide of battle in favor of the bandits unless their configuration was broken. Doug came erect and moved swiftly toward them.

Before he had taken three steps, a barbaric cry split

the night, and, for an instant, seemed to freeze all the fighting figures in place. Doug pulled up short. A giant near-naked figure rushed maniacally upon the quartet of bandits. They hesitated, stunned by the cry. Then Cortozca was among them like a maniac.

A bleeding body was hurled a dozen feet by a single sweep of his great stone club. Gunfire stabbed at him from point-blank range. Another bandit reeled away screaming. Even Doug's trained eye could not follow the furious whirl of action after that.

Then, incredibly, Cortozca stood alone and unharmed amidst the broken bodies at his feet. He bent and snatched an object from a dying hand. Triumphantly, he lifted aloft a lever-action rifle. His Devil Dusted eyes flamed in a wild ecstasy. He thrust the rifle high overhead.

Movement to Doug's right tore his attention from that scene and its significance. He wheeled, throwing up his club by reflex. It intercepted the wild downward stroke of the sword intended to split his skull. The bandit jumped back. Doug saw his weapon fully for the first time. It was a long, curved, cavalry-type saber of antique vintage, too heavy for most men to wield comfortably one-handed.

The desperado's face was savage. He sprang back in to the attack. He had no trouble at all handling the blade. Doug blocked left, with his club held at an angle. He flipped it over to intercept another slash from his right. Steel grated on stone. Doug drove the blunt top of the war club's head straight out into the swordsman's face. He then swung to cut him down.

Demented, savage laughter mingled with two gunshots jerked Doug's head around. He saw a towering fat figure topped by a battered sombrero. The figure's foot was upraised above a writhing, wounded warrior. El Demonio stomped down brutally, and then a second time. The warrior's struggles stopped. The bandit chieftain brayed triumphant laughter. In one fist he gripped a smoking revolver. In the other he brandished a long machete.

Doug rushed him from behind. He had no compunction at striking this brute down from the rear. Some atavistic sense warned El Demonio. He whirled his massive body about with shocking speed. His ugly face lit up as he saw Doug coming. He rushed to meet him.

It was like being charged by a dinosaur. Doug faltered. He tried to fling himself aside. He was too slow. El Demonio's bulk smashed bruisingly into him. He was knocked flat. His club sailed from his hands. The night sky reeled overhead. Harsh, mad laughter rang in his ears. Through pain-blurred eyes he saw El Demonio point the big revolver down at him.

Doug levered himself up on his palms and left foot in a desperate surge. His right foot snapped out and caught the revolver. It blasted skyward and cartwheeled from the bandit's hand. El Demonio lifted a massive booted foot and stomped down at Doug's chest. Doug glimpsed sharp caulks studding the boot sole, like the boot of a lumberjack. It rammed agonizingly down into his chest. He was driven flat. El Demonio ground the boot down, pinning him like a bug.

High above him, silhouetted against the wild night sky, towered the bloated shape of the brute. The long machete flashed up in the firelight. On his back, his chest being crushed, Doug swung one leg up in a desperate kick. At the height of its arc, his foot drove into the small of El Demonio's back. The mad laughter spawned a belch. El Demonio lurched forward.

From his bench-press position, Doug caught the heavy boot on his chest and thrust it twistingly up. On one foot, El Demonio hopped absurdly sideways. But he caught his balance and slashed the machete down.

Doug rolled. The blade bit deep into the ground where he had lain. He came up onto his feet, dagger in hand. His chest felt on fire. El Demonio bellowed laughter and swung the machete down from overhead. His face, framed by the sombrero and greasy mane of hair, was horrifying.

Doug thrust the stone dagger up. The weight of the machete stroke against it bent his arm down. El Demonio looped the machete around at his rib cage from his left. Again Doug interposed stone to metal. He could not continue this absurd fencing match. A single misjudgment and the machete would finish him.

El Demonio cut down at the juncture of his neck

and shoulder. This time Doug used his left arm to block. He snapped it up to meet a wrist that felt like a rod of steel beneath a layer of fat. With his right hand, Doug drove the stone dagger deep into El Demonio's fat belly.

El Demonio bellowed. Doug stabbed again, then a third time. He sprang clear. El Demonio turned around. His arm dropped, and the machete fell from his fingers. He clutched his middle and fell to his knees. He began to laugh. It was a horrible, lost sound that echoed in the night. Still laughing, he fell forward on his face and died.

Doug wilted to one knee. Perhaps the leader of the desperadoes really had been a demon out of hell.

Around him, he realized, the sounds of battle were slackening. The bandits were breaking off the conflict. The savagery of the unexpected attack had been too much for them. And the death of their leader had been noted, adding to their demoralization. Doug watched as the warriors cut down the fleeing desperadoes. Only a few escaped into the darkness. Doug hoped that the women had been among them.

The mood was one of triumph. The stores of the bandit camp were ransacked and a victory feast began. Among the stores were cheap whiskey and crude beer. Before morning, at least half of the warriors had imbibed to the point of drunkenness.

Doug sat alone at the edge of the camp. He had not touched the alcohol. He was pleased to note that the majority of the drunken revelers bore the plesiosaur tattoo. Most of the Queen's men had remained sober.

His chest burned as if a shovelful of red-hot coals had been jammed against it, although the wound left by El Demonio's caulked boot was not really serious. He had found the Quaztar equivalent of a field medic to apply a soothing salve that eased the pain somewhat.

Cortozca began to rouse the sullen warriors as the sky behind the mountains grew lighter. He spotted Doug and approached with the arrogant stride of a leader victorious in battle. Much of the yellow fire had faded from his eyes.

"The Queen's Warrior has won a mighty victory," Doug greeted him.

Cortozca surveyed the camp with satisfaction. "It was worthwhile," he said. His eyes came back to Doug. "You killed El Demonio."

"Not before he almost killed me."

"They say he was a mighty fighter."

"Now he's a dead one."

Cortozca grunted and walked away. Doug watched the retreat of his mighty figure. He remembered Cortozca's awesome prowess in battle and his lifting high of the captured rifle. Something in Cortozca's comment about the battle pricked him with unease.

The camp was stirring, but it would still be some hours, he guessed, before the warriors were in any sort of shape to begin the return march. He had lost track of Cortozca. The pricking ran up and down his spine. The Queen's Warrior bore watching.

Rising to his feet, Doug scanned the surrounding peaks. He noted an outthrusting ledge that promised a clear overview of the camp. No one appeared to notice as he clambered up among the rocks to reach it.

The sun rose, its rays striking the mountains with fiery splendor. To Doug's side, the wall of a cliff plunged a hundred feet sheer into a crevasse where the snow never melted. How deep was it? What lay buried in its depths? He pulled his thoughts away.

Even from his vantage point he found it hard to keep track of Cortozca as the warrior organized his men. Doug fingered the rough stone of his club and glanced down into the crevasse. When he looked back at the camp, he frowned as he scanned it. The Queen's Warrior was nowhere in evidence.

A foot slid on stone behind him. He turned as he rose, bringing up his club. His eyes blazing with yellow fire, Cortozca brought his own war club sweeping down toward him.

Doug had his club only half raised. Stone shattered beneath Cortozca's stroke. The fragments of Doug's club sprayed like shrapnel. Cortozca gave a growling roar. He swung his club again. Doug had no choice. He flung himself backward into the crevasse.

Chapter Eight

"**Y**our Doug is an exceptional man." Tanztra's voice was almost teasing.

"*My* Doug?" Ellen protested. She was sure that she couldn't quite hide her pleasure at the attribution.

Tanztra smiled warmly. "Come now, sister, it is evident that the fire burns between you and Doug. I almost envy you."

Ellen felt a flush spread across her face. "There are good men among your warriors," she ventured. "Dalzar, for instance, feels something more than a subject's devotion for you, I think."

The Queen sighed. "You are right," she conceded. "Perhaps the fire would burn between us, too, if I would but let it."

"Why don't you?"

"I fear for his life if I do. In rejecting Cortozca as my husband, I have earned his enmity toward any man I would so honor. If it were other than Cortozca, I would not fear for Dalzar to confront him. But no man can stand against Cortozca."

Tanztra's loneliness echoed bleakly in her words. Ellen thought of the giant warrior and shuddered. In a very real way, Cortozca was more terrifying than the plesiosaur in the lake. The beast was only an animal, but Cortozca's motives were all too human. "I'll be glad when Doug's back," she said. She would not allow herself to consider the alternative.

"As will I. The war party has been gone nearly two days now. They should return in the morning." Now it was she who shuddered. "There have been strange sounds in the cavern at night. People have heard eerie cries and wailing. And it is said that the god has emerged from the waters to prowl in the night. Never before has this happened."

Tanztra's personal maid had appeared. She said, "One of the new warriors awaits an audience with the Maiden Adviser."

One of the new warriors? Ellen thought. She had not seen Dick since Doug left. She looked appealingly at Tanztra, who nodded approval. Ellen rose and hurried after the maid.

Dick awaited her just within the entry to the Queen's chambers.

"Dick!" She went to him in a little rush, but drew up short as full awareness of his strange demeanor struck her. This was a different Dick from the man with whom she had so recently shared a special closeness.

His field clothes were tattered and worn. They were little better than rags. His face was dirty, his hands begrimed. His eyes glittered with fatigue held rigidly in check. What in the world had he been doing? she wondered.

"Ellen." His voice was hoarse. His hand dropped to caress his computer, which, along with the walkie-talkie, still hung on his belt.

"Are you all right?" she managed to ask through her shock.

"Yes!" he snapped, then seemed to catch himself. "I need to see you." He glanced significantly at the hovering maid. "Alone."

"Of course." She followed him into the corridor. She could not help flinching from his unwashed odor. It frightened her a little. The Dickinson Tyler she had known and idolized had always been fastidious in his personal habits, even in the field.

He led her down the passage to a secluded niche. His stride was jerky. He turned abruptly once they were out of sight of the door to Tanztra's chambers.

"Where have you been?" Ellen asked. "I've been worried about you."

"Have you?" His tone carried an edge of mockery.

"Of course." Suddenly she felt as awkward as if she were facing a grim and somehow threatening stranger.

"I've been conducting research. In the cave." Again he stroked his computer as if it were a talisman. "You can't imagine the things I've learned, the power I've discovered." He broke off abruptly as if fearful of saying more than he wanted to. "I need to share it with you."

She disregarded his remarks. "I've been worried to death about you!"

His expression hardened, and he said scornfully, "I wouldn't have thought that you had time for any concern for my well-being, what with making girl-talk with the Queen and throwing yourself at Bonner."

"Throwing myself at him?" she gasped, stung. "That's not true, Dick. But even if it was, it wouldn't be any concern of yours."

He winced as if she had clawed him, but she could not really regret the words or the truth they expressed.

"I thought that after all we had experienced together, we were more than simple acquaintances," he said stiffly.

"You've been my teacher and friend, and—and my confidant, but I've never led you to believe there was anything more between us." She could feel the tears streaming down her face. Why was he doing this?

His stiff formality cracked. "Bonner is a savage, a barbarian," he said vehemently. "He's no better than those drug dealers. Did you see how quickly he fit into this uncivilized tribe?"

"Dick!" she cried. "*I* fit in here better than I do in a lot of places back in the so-called civilized world. Tanztra is the best friend I've ever had. And it's not right for you to say those things about Doug. He's saved our lives. He saved *your* life!"

For a moment he stared beyond her into some dark realm. "Okay," he said, "you've made your position plain."

"Dick, wait!" She tried to catch his arm as he brushed past her. He shrugged her off with unexpected strength. Helpless, she stared after him as he strode away.

Dazedly, she started back down the corridor. His cruel words repeated themselves in her mind. It was a few moments before she realized there was a figure lurking just outside the Queen's chambers. She could not mistake the sinister form of Simon, or the stubby shape of the automatic weapon gripped expertly in his hands. Intent on the doorway, Simon was clearly not aware of her presence.

Quickly, she pulled out Doug's .45 from under her clothing and extended it in the two-handed stance he had shown her.

"What are you doing here?" she yelled.

Simon whirled with a lithe, catlike quickness. The ugly little barrel of his stubby assault gun swung toward her.

She fired, and fired again and again and again with a curious sense of remote concentration. Simon was falling. The reverberations of her shots chased her yell down the hallways.

Numb with horror, she let herself slump against the wall. The .45 was still clenched tightly in her hands. Its slide was locked back. She had fired every shot in it. She was only vaguely aware of Tanztra emerging from her chambers to rush to her, and of the sudden appearance of Dalzar and other warriors. Dalzar's revelation of a guard slain from behind seemed to reach her from a great distance. She comprehended dully that Simon had been on a mission of assassination against the Queen and, most likely, herself. She huddled against the wall in Tanztra's arms and prayed for Doug's return.

The coldness had swallowed Doug completely. Perversely, it had somehow made him warm. Could a person be warm and cold at the same time? How could he feel this curious, warm lassitude through the awful cold that chilled him to his soul?

The answer to that question stirred distressingly in some distant segment of his mind. The final stage of death by freezing was reputed to be a sense of warmth and comfort. A person could feel warm when literally freezing to death.

Doug stirred and flailed sluggishly. He clawed his way up out of the darkness and the enveloping pressure. Daylight blinded him. He was floundering half buried in the snow that filled the bottom of the crevasse. It had broken his fall, as he had prayed it would, but the impact had knocked him senseless and buried him in its yielding depths.

He lurched and fought his way to a narrow ledge, then pulled himself clear of the snow.

For a while he lay still. Then he forced himself to a sitting position and began to rub his limbs to restore circulation. Once clear of the snow, there was less danger of freezing to death, but he was still cold.

The afternoon was well along. Apparently Cortozca had been content to leave him for dead. It had not been an unreasonable conclusion to reach, he thought wryly.

The side of the crevasse offered easy hand grasps and footholds, but he climbed cautiously, alert for the sounds of human presence. There were none. He emerged from the crevasse and looked down on the bandit encampment. It was inhabited by scurrying rats, feeding condors, and the bodies of the dead. Cortozca and his war party were gone.

He clambered stiffly down to the camp. Rats darted away from him. The huge condors took to the air with shrill resentment. Doug also prowled the camp like a scavenger. If he was to survive, he needed a weapon other than the stone dagger still sheathed at his waist.

He realized after the third body that there were no guns left in the camp. The realization brought a chill to the back of his neck. Cortozca had achieved his goal. This raid had not been so much for vengeance as to obtain firearms for his men. True, most of the guns were primitive, but they would give their users a great advantage over foemen armed with stone clubs and daggers.

He guessed that Cortozca had not been obvious in

collecting the weapons. He would not have wanted to alert the warriors loyal to the Queen that his men were now armed with firearms. Most likely, he had sent back a squad of his own warriors to secure the weapons. Or, perhaps, they had simply waited behind on the pretext of looking for him, Doug.

The image of Cortozca lifting the captured rifle high came to Doug's mind. He recalled the warrior's cryptic comment about the value of the raid. Cortozca's motives should have been obvious to him. With firearms in the hands of his warriors, Cortozca would waste no time in launching his long-planned coup attempt. He would not have the time or the ammunition for extensive training efforts that would prematurely reveal his possession of the guns to Tanztra. But even in untrained hands, the firearms would give his forces an insurmountable advantage.

A discarded war club caught his eye. He picked it up. As he did, he remembered the guard he had killed the night before. He hurried to the place where he had left the body. It was undisturbed. Eagerly he went past it to the rocks.

The AK-47 was still where he had hidden it. He snatched it up. The search of the camp had missed the assault rifle. He returned to the body of the weapon's owner. Obviously unarmed, the body had not been searched. Doug bared his teeth in satisfaction as he found the loaded magazine on the body. With a clip already in the gun, he now had two.

A tattered rope had been attached to the rifle as

a sling. He hung it on one shoulder and found another piece of rope to make a crude sling for his club. The two weapons—ancient and modern—clicked together as he shrugged the slings into place.

His remaining preparations were few. He appropriated a battered canteen and filled it with water from a nearby spring. He found some nonperishable foodstuffs that would go into his small ration bag along with the jerked meat he already carried. He gnawed hungrily at a strip of the meat as he left camp. He had only a few hours of daylight left, and he doubted that he could travel at night. He wanted to get as much use as he could out of the time he had. He wondered how far ahead of him the war party was.

Retracing the trail was easy at first. He ignored the exhaustion pressuring him. His thoughts revolved around Ellen. What would she feel when the war party returned with the report of his disappearance in the mountains? What would be her fate if Cortozca and Mixtek were successful in their coup? He quickened his pace.

He stopped only when the darkness made it impossible to see. He spent the long night huddled beneath a stone overhang. It was bitterly cold, but the stone niche trapped some of his body heat. Exhaustion finally pulled him down into sleep.

In the light of morning he looked out over a vast expanse of stony wilderness beneath a bluing sky. He hitched the gun and club into comfortable positions and left the overhang behind.

Ahead of him the trail was little more than an outward bulge across a sheer cliff face. He eyed it dubiously before edging cautiously out onto it. His spread-eagled body was pressed to the hard stone. High above him, the black wall of the cliff towered until it appeared to lean precariously out over him. At his back, a panoramic void of mountains and sky seemed to revolve. He concentrated on the cliff face, inches in front of his eyes.

He felt it first through the stone itself. A vibration was transmitted to his gripping fingers. His nerve ends tingled. Instinct tensed his muscles.

Then the wall of rock shimmied like the body of some great beast shaking itself. An earth tremor! The stone surface seemed to thrust itself outward as if to shove him from his perch. He felt the whole mountain shift. He tried to dig his fingers into the stone. The vibrations rattled his teeth. He felt as though the entire cliff face had been tilted so that he clung like a fly upside down above the reeling void. A horrified nausea clawed within him.

Gradually the cliff face seemed to tilt back to the vertical, and the vibrations faded away into the depths of the stone. Doug began to breathe again.

Then, once again, the stone began to vibrate. But it was a different type of vibration this time. A roaring came down out of the sky. Doug tilted his head back, stared upward, and gasped. Dislodged by the quake, a great mass of stone and rubble was plunging down the cliff face toward him.

Desperately he scrambled sideward back the way he had come. He could not fling himself clear. He would never regain a perch on the wall. Like the landslide, he would go plummeting into the abyss.

Stones pelted him. The down-rushing mass seemed to obliterate the sky. Then there was no more time to move. He could only hug the cliff face in desperation and pray that he had made it out of the path of the slide.

Its roar was all around him. Its darkness enveloped him. Something bounced hard from his shoulder and almost took him from his perch. Something else struck his leg. Rushing air tore at him. He buried his face against the unyielding stone and held on with all his strength and will. Dust choked him and the world itself seemed to end.

The eternal roar faded, and the last rush of displaced air tugged at him. A few small stones and pebbles bounced past. Doug forced his eyes open. He blinked against the dust and peered cautiously upward. It was over. He had been far enough to the outside so that only the edge of the landslide had brushed him.

He spat dirt from his mouth and looked about. His spirit shrank within him. The pathway was gone. The landslide had torn a great scar down the face of the cliff, obliterating the precarious trail.

Doug's arms began to tremble. He gritted his teeth

and willed himself to coolness. He craned his neck to look up and down the face of the cliff. The trail was gone, but the massive stretch of scarred and torn stone left in the wake of the avalanche offered a multitude of hand- and footholds. Looking up and beyond the scar, Doug thought he detected a narrow ledge that would offer a means of progressing. He could not afford to go back and seek a new route. He wouldn't reach Quaztar in time. He might not do so even now.

Gingerly he edged to the point where the trail ended. It seemed a wide pathway to him now. He reached out and up for a small projection of stone with his right hand. Gripping it, he lifted his right foot and wedged it into a shallow cleft. For an instant he closed his eyes. Then he pulled himself up off the path. He shifted hands and groped for another handhold. Finding one, he wedged his left foot against stone and drew himself up until his right foot found purchase again.

He went on like that, a groping, clinging process that moved him slowly up and across the face of the scar. He blinked sweat from his eyes. Twinges and tinglings twitched his muscles like electrical charges.

A cold wind blew down out of the sky and threatened to pluck him from the cliff face. He closed his eyes against it. Opening them, he inadvertently looked down. The world spread away below him. He guessed that the ground was at least a mile beneath him. He pictured himself clinging like some insect to the vast vertical plane of the wall.

His hand did not want to release its hold. He forced himself to reach up for the next grip. His hand was trembling. Of their own volition, his eyes sought the madness of the void beneath him. He closed them rather than look down again. The wind snatched at him with icy talons.

He felt his fingers close on a projection of stone. He made his eyes open and made his body begin the laborious process of inching upward once more.

He felt the stone break loose in his hand. As his right foot slipped free from its purchase, he swung out over the abyss, supported for an unending instant only by his left hand and left foot. The enormous spectacle of mountains stretching to the horizon blurred before his vision. He yelled with anger and fear into the teeth of the wind. Instinctively he arched his body, and then felt himself swing back into the cliff face. For a moment he was sure that he hung there by raw willpower alone.

Then his scrabbling right hand found a new hold, and his foot came to rest on a thread of a ledge. He urged himself to go on. If he stopped now, he knew he would not move again until his muscles betrayed him and he plunged into the void.

He clawed his way up to a new ledge and kept going from there. It did not get easier. But his mind reached a kind of overload, fading the insane horror of his situation from consciousness. Like an automaton he reached and clutched with his hands, kicked and scrabbled with his feet, used the wearied muscles of his legs and arms and back to lift and thrust himself up and across the vertical plane of stone.

When his straining foot at last found purchase on the ledge he was seeking, he did not believe his achievement. Even when he huddled on the narrow expanse of stone and looked back across the scarred course of the landslide, he did not believe it.

He crouched there until his mind meshed once more with reality. Finally he rose on shaky legs. He found that he could actually walk along the ledge, though in a cautious fashion. After the nightmare of the cliff face it was like a highway.

It did not run far, however, and it ended abruptly in a narrow cleft in the rock. Doug surveyed the cliff beyond the end of the ledge. It was as sheer as glass, and with no handholds. Reluctantly he ducked into the darkness of the cleft.

He saw light ahead of him. A foul, acrid odor burned his nostrils. A strange cackling floated down the length of the narrow passage. Belatedly he thought to unsling the rifle, but the cleft was too narrow for arm movement.

Stepping out into the open, he had a brief impression of a large rookery some sixty feet in diameter at the bottom of an equally wide chimney of rock. Blue sky was far overhead. Great avian shapes rose up like demons before him. They spread wide their huge black wings.

Doug realized that he had stumbled into a cluster of nesting condors. Feathers, droppings, and more than a dozen of their large, ragged nests were scattered about the rookery. The voracious, ugly heads of young birds strained upward from several of the nests.

The nearest adult bird lurched toward him, its ten-foot wings spread as if to envelop him. Erect, it was almost as tall as he. Its bald head darted toward him with a gaping beak. He dodged back. Behind it, he could see others of the monstrous birds shuffling ominously forward.

Doug read the danger. The condors were normally scavengers, giant vultures preying on the dead. Now, alarmed by the earlier quake, their territory violated, they would attack him en masse without hesitation. Their beaks could strip dead flesh from bone. And they could do the same to living flesh.

Doug shifted sideways. The raucous cries of the birds deafened him. The stench seared his nostrils. He had an instant's view of the black mouth of a low tunnel across the width of the rookery. He did not know to where it led, but if he turned back, he would only be trapped on the ledge again.

The nearest bird struck at him again. He had no desire to injure them. He was the invader in their domain. Mankind had driven their North American cousins into virtual extinction.

He struck out at the bobbing head with his fist— a good right cross. His knuckles scraped against the horny beak. The condor lurched dazedly away. Doug unlimbered the AK-47 with a single shrug. The stock and bayonet were still folded. Flailing it left and right, he charged at the snapping beaks, whirling feathers, and buffeting wings. Taloned feet groped awkwardly at his ankles and legs. He ducked a darting beak, batted another aside with the rifle. A flapping wing caught him jarringly across his face. He tasted foul feathers. Desperately he swiveled his torso back and forth, gun held horizontally before him, and plunged forward.

He broke through their ranks. Some of them were launching clumsily into the air. The thought of taloned feet and clashing beaks descending on him from above was a horror. He hurtled a six-foot nest. The infant birds raised their gaping beaks as he flashed over them.

Another condor seemed to rise out of the rock. He glimpsed savage eyes behind its flashing beak. He hurled it aside with a sweep of his left arm. It let out an enraged squawk.

Doug lunged down to his knees. Crawling, shoving the rifle ahead of him, he scrabbled into the tunnel mouth while a slashing beak grazed his heel.

He scrambled forward several yards over a rough stony surface. Behind him the shrieks and calls of the outraged condors diminished. He stopped for a moment to gather his resources. Once again there was no going back. It was only by the grace of God that he had come through his ordeals with no serious wounds. What kind of diseases did the condors carry? Shuddering, he put the thought from him. He might not even live long enough to find out.

He was in some kind of flaw that snaked its way through the solid rock of the cliff. It was barely high enough for him to crawl forward. He unfolded the flimsy bayonet on the AK-47 and used it to probe ahead of him into the darkness. On hands and knees, poking the bayonet before him, he advanced.

Eventually, the tunnel angled upward. Doug squeezed past and around rocky protuberances as he ascended. Occasionally he jabbed the bayonet overhead. Often it scraped on rock. The darkness pressed down on him from below and above. Climbing was relatively easy, because his back was usually pressed tight against the wall. He was like a worm in a hole. He pushed himself upward, and his shoulders wedged firmly in the passage. He shoved harder and felt himself slide upward a few inches before he stuck firm again. The hand holding his rifle was thrust overhead. His other arm was pressed tightly to his body. The war club dug painfully into his back. He was entombed alive, he thought, trapped here until Judgment Day, which would find only his bones still wedged in this eternal, suffocating darkness. Panic flared in him. He kicked with his feet and scrabbled at the unyielding stone. His body would not budge.

Panting, he rested. He could feel the tingling in both arms as their circulation was cut off. What would happen if another tremor came while he was in this tunnel? Would the stone walls shift together, smashing him into oblivion? Better the flaying beaks of the condors than that grisly fate. He groped for rationality. If need be, he told himself, he could go back once he had gotten loose. Despite his reluctance, he could use the AK-47 on the birds and somehow retrace his progress and seek a new route.

But not yet, he decided.

He exhaled, forcing all the air from his lungs. He began to writhe and wriggle, compacting his torso with mental and physical effort. He got good purchase with both feet and shoved hard. He felt his body skin upward an inch. He worked his torso back and forth, berating the club pressing into his back. He groped with the hand trapped against him and made contact with the side of the tunnel. It gave him extra leverage, and he shoved himself upward. His other hand, still clutching the rifle, hooked over a knob of stone. He pulled and kicked and fought his way free.

Doggedly he continued to climb. He began to believe that he had been in this dark, harrowing tunnel since the beginning of time and would remain there until its end. Once he thought that something pursued him. It scrabbled and scratched as it sought to reach him from below. He climbed faster. The sounds—if he had actually heard them—faded below him. He did not want to consider what might have been pursuing him in the depth of the earth.

Gradually the tunnel returned to the horizontal.

Once again he crawled and writhed on knees, elbows, and belly through its narrow confines. Suddenly he detected a lessening of the impenetrable darkness. At first he refused to accept it and the hope it sparked within him. But there came a point when he was actually able to discern the rough contours of the tunnel. With new strength he forced his tired body forward.

Chapter Nine

Doug emerged from the tunnel on a rocky slope beneath a noon sky. He ducked his head and shielded his eyes until they were accustomed to the daylight. Blinking, he peered out across the landscape and said a prayer of thanks. Two miles away, past a barren ridge, was a rounded peak he recognized from the journey to the bandits' camp. His subterranean wanderings had not taken him too deeply into unfamiliar territory. Quaztar itself was not far distant beyond the rounded mountain.

He moved out at a long, striding pace. Jogging was impossible in this terrain. It felt good to be breathing fresh air and to be able to move freely, unconstricted by rock.

At the base of the rounded peak he found the trail along which Cortozca had led the war party two days before. Cortozca and his victorious warriors would have reached Quaztar by now. What was happening there? He tried not to dwell on the various scenarios that came to mind.

147

How would Cortozca explain his absence? The Queen's Warrior had not actually seen his death. Apparently he had been satisfied that the fall into the crevasse was the finish of him. Doug came to an abrupt halt. Had Cortozca really been satisfied that he was dead? With the firearms at hand, he would not have wanted to waste time searching for him. And, if Cortozca wasn't satisfied that he was dead, what precautions might he have taken against his return?

Doug considered the question. On the chance that his enemy might have survived, Cortozca could well have set a trap for him. More slowly, Doug resumed his progress. Any trap by Cortozca would have only limited manpower, because he would want his forces at full strength for the takeover attempt. Hence, the trap would need to be at a spot that Doug was likely to pass on his return. Doug recalled a narrow divide that led into the valley through the barrier cliffs. He nodded with grim certainty. It was there that death would be awaiting him. If he could avoid doing so, he would not use the AK-47. His ammunition was limited, and its sound might alert other unseen watchers to his return.

The divide through the mountains was nearly a mile long and over a hundred yards wide at its mouth, he recalled. It narrowed steadily downward until it debouched into the valley. Jagged, rocky walls overlooked the entrance into the valley itself.

Doug paused in concealment to observe the wide

mouth of the pass. Tendrils of the drifting fog caressed his face with clammy touches. He detected nothing significant. Moving into the open, he mounted into the rocky foothills and peaks through which the passage cut. He paralleled the course of the divide, even though the going was slower than it would have been on the floor of the pass. He held himself to a wary pace.

As he entered fully into the mist, the rock walls of the divide carried the echoes of men's voices through the fog. He moved forward like a wraith. The voices, heightened by moist air, grew louder and more distinct. He caught an obscene reference to the stupidity of their assignment to watch the pass. Apparently his would-be ambushers had little faith that he would be returning. He would make that lack of faith their undoing.

Silently he mounted a great oblong boulder. From it, he could look down twenty feet onto his enemies. Five warriors lounged irritably behind the concealment of a jumble of boulders. Anything that moved along the divide would have to pass by them.

"This is fool's work," one of them said.

"You tell Cortozca that," another jeered. "I'll pick up your pieces for your woman."

The first speaker insisted, "The interloper is dead."

"You just wish I was," Doug said.

The five of them scrambled about to stare up at him. Doug saw their shocked pale faces and their blue-tattooed foreheads.

"Kill him!" several shouted. They scrambled up the steep slope, clubs raised.

Doug hopped down behind the shelter of the great oblong boulder. He dug the butt of his club in under its edge. The club was a Quaztar war club. As a lever now, it was ideal. Doug heaved against it. His muscles bunched and strained. The boulder was twelve feet long and nearly half that in height. Balanced on the ledge, it rocked forward. Doug stretched his body and shoved upward on his makeshift lever with all his power.

He felt the boulder tilt. His temples pounded as he heaved. He could hear the savage cries of the ascending warriors on the far side of the boulder. In moments they would scramble over and be atop him. Then the whole huge rock lurched forward. Its weight slipped off the lever. Doug staggered back a pace. Like a juggernaut, the boulder rolled down upon the attacking warriors. Their screams mingled with its rumble. The ground trembled beneath Doug's feet. Then came the crash of impact with the ground. The last of the screams stopped abruptly.

The five warriors had been trapped between the boulder and the pile of stones that had concealed them. Doug did not look too closely at the carnage. He continued through the mist to the entrance into the valley.

The echoes of the falling stone had faded. In the distance Doug heard the faint popping of gunfire. He began to run.

* * *

"I don't like this, my ladies." Dalzar fingered the haft of his club tensely.

"Nor do I, Dalzar," Tanztra admitted. She stood very close to the tall warrior. "This is a strange ceremony Mixtek has called. I have never seen its like."

Ellen barely heard their exchange. Her mind still felt numbed by shock and grief and outrage. And her eyes were red from weeping. The harsh chanting of Mixtek atop the altar beside the temple seemed remote and unrelated to her. She would not—could not—accept that Doug was dead. Cortozca's brief explanation of Doug's disappearance in the mountains was not enough. There had to be more.

"I've told our warriors to hold themselves separate from those of the High Priest," Dalzar was saying. "And to be alert for any signal from me. I've also assigned a group to guard the entrance here to the temple."

The tension in his voice penetrated Ellen's despair. She looked out over the ranks of warriors from her position with the Queen and Dalzar atop the temple. She could see the separation that Dalzar had ordered. Like opposing forces, the two crowds of warriors faced each other uneasily.

Mixtek's unnerving chant droned on. He had called for the ceremony shortly after the war party's victorious return. Only the warriors and the ruling officials were to attend. The ceremony was purportedly in honor of the warriors. Ellen guessed that virtually all the warriors were present. The High Priest had not used the horn that summoned the plesiosaur, for which Ellen had breathed a prayer of thanks. There were to be no sacrifices on the giant altar. The dark waters swirled sluggishly.

Ellen studied the ranks of warriors as she searched for Dick's presence. Though named a warrior, he was not in sight below, and she hadn't seen him since their painful exchange prior to the assassination attempt by Simon. Confronted, Aguilar, Simon's master, had insisted that the gunman had acted without his knowledge. Mixtek had declared the drug lord exempt from punishment for the attack.

And now this bizarre ceremony, Ellen thought, growing more troubled. What purpose did it serve?

Her eyes fell on the imposing Cortozca. The Queen's Warrior towered among the foremost ranks of his forces. Even in that savage company he stood out in barbaric magnificence. His eyes were eerily ablaze with an unnatural yellow fire. Something in the stiffness of his stance and those of the warriors immediately around him was unusual, she thought. She noted again that most of the front rank of tattooed warriors wore long capes. In her brief experience here, the capes were unusual attire for warriors.

Cortozca looked sharply to his left and right. As he snapped both arms straight overhead, there was a stirring among his frontline warriors.

"Dalzar!" Ellen said sharply.

He turned toward her, his expression questioning.

Below, Cortozca brought his arms sweeping down. Ellen saw the horribly familiar shape of the sawed-off shotgun that the warrior next to Cortozca drew from beneath his cape. The ceremony was a ruse. It was meant as a death trap for Tanztra's warriors.

"*No!*" she screamed. Her voice flung strident echoes throughout the cavern, drowning even Mixtek's chant. It slowed Cortozca's men in producing their unfamiliar weapons.

Dalzar sprang to her side. He assessed the situation with a single sweep of his gaze. A gunshot rang out. Ellen thought it went wild. Uncertainty rippled through the ranks of both masses of warriors. Cortozca bellowed commands, urging his forces to the attack. He snatched the shotgun from the hands of the nearest warrior. He triggered it and an opposing warrior fell. The two crowds of warriors swayed together. More gunshots sounded. War clubs flashed high.

Dalzar whirled away from the parapet of the temple roof. "My ladies!" he snapped. "Get below into the temple! The men I stationed here will guard the entrance. Cortozca and a number of his men have firearms. We cannot oppose them in the open. I will lead a withdrawal into the ruins, which will give us cover. We will fight them there. Quick now!"

He hurried them down the stairway into an interior chamber of the building. He raced away along its corridors. Outside, the sounds of battle grew louder. Ellen looked at Tanztra and saw the fear in the Queen's dark eyes.

Doug gazed down on violence and madness. Crouched atop masonry on the outer edge of the ruined cavern city, he had a commanding view of the lake and the ruins. Cortozca's coup attempt was well under way. Doug saw pale figures ducking and dodging through the ruins in the eerie light of the Fire Lichen. Occasional gunfire sounded.

Cortozca was meeting stiff resistance from the warriors loyal to the Queen. Apparently the latter group had retreated into the ruins and were waging a guerrilla war against their better-armed opponents. The rebel warriors' inexperience with their firearms prevented the weapons from being the great asset they would have been in the hands of trained modern soldiers. Some warriors clashed in close-in fighting with only clubs and daggers. Not all of Cortozca's troops were armed with guns.

He searched for Cortozca, but could not spot him. In front of the temple, two smaller groups of warriors were locked in combat. From atop the altar, Mixtek exhorted one group. The priest's arms waved wildly. Out on the lake, Doug could see the ceaseless movement of the water.

He laid his club aside and checked the AK-47. It had come through his ordeals in good shape, and he was glad he hadn't used ammunition on the condors. A large chunk of masonry made a good sniper's rest.

He set the selector to single fire. He did not want to go to full automatic unless he had no other choice.

He put the sights on the torso of a skulking warrior armed with a heavy revolver. At least initially, he would have little trouble distinguishing his targets, he reflected grimly. He had never cared for long-distance killing.

He squeezed the trigger, and across the cavern the warrior pivoted and fell. The sights were dead on, Doug realized with hard-edged satisfaction. He shifted his aim to a second target and fired again. The crack of the AK-47 was lost in the vastness of the cavern and the uproar of battle. His target plunged backward out of sight. Another warrior nearby looked startled. Doug could actually see the tattoo on his forehead. He knocked him over too.

As yet, there was no alarm over his presence. The warriors had never been exposed to sniper fire before and would be slow to recognize it for what it was. Doug sought another target, but missed as the man darted forward and disappeared into a building. He could not afford many misses, he berated himself.

Two warriors grappled in close combat. Doug held on them until the larger man tripped the other and knelt with an upraised dagger. Doug sighted on the blue tattoo and took him down. The rescued warrior sat up and looked around in bewilderment. Then he scrambled to rejoin the fighting.

Doug continued to pick his targets. He hit more than he missed. As warriors of the Queen realized that they were receiving unexpected assistance, they fought with renewed fervor. Doug saw three tattooed warriors go down beneath the clubs and daggers of Tanztra's men. His own targets became more scarce. The enemy warriors were beginning to understand that death stalked them from afar. Doug changed magazines. For the moment he could spot no clear targets. He had lost track of how many men he had taken out of action.

Doug swung the sight across his killing field. Suddenly a score of warriors sprang into sight. Behind them moved an unmistakable giant figure—Cortozca. Doug snapped a shot—and knew he had fired too fast. Cortozca disappeared. The twenty warriors charged Doug.

Obviously, his location had been spotted and Cortozca had ordered an attack. Howling, discharging what weapons they had, the warriors rushed across the cavern floor toward his position.

Coolly, Doug centered on a lead warrior brandishing an old lever action. The AK-47 slug punched him backward. Doug shifted his aim and fired again, and then once more. Three down. The charge did not break. The warriors came rushing on. They would be on him before he could pick them off one by one.

Full automatic then. No choice. Doug flicked the selector, then rose to his feet and braced the assault rifle at waist level. The attackers were almost at the base of his mound. He pressed the trigger back and swept bullets across their ranks. Thunder hammered

in his fists. Hot brass rained at his feet. Oncoming
warriors stumbled and reeled as the spray of lead
raked across them.

The rifle ran empty in Doug's hands. Six remaining warriors stormed up the mound to reach him.

Doug stepped forward and kicked. The foremost
attacker's head snapped back, and he toppled limply
into a pair of his comrades. The other three warriors
reached the mound's summit. Two were on Doug's
left, one on his right. None had firearms. Doug could
not reach his club. In moments the other two would
be upon him also.

A stone dagger skewered in front of him from his
right. He drove the butt of the AK-47 hard in that
direction. The Chinese version was not meant for this
kind of combat, and the flimsy metal stock crumpled
with the impact. But the warrior reeled away and collapsed, clutching his middle.

The other two warriors impeded each other. Doug
ducked an awkwardly swung club. He stamped down
on an instep, wishing momentarily for El Demonio's
caulked boots. Bone collapsed under his foot. The
warrior gasped. Twisting sideways, Doug turned the
assault rifle vertical, catching a swing of the other
warrior's club. The rifle shivered in his hands. The
banana clip popped free. Doug gripped the gun with
his right hand around the pistol grip, then lunged like
a fencer. The weight of the rifle was awkward in his
one-handed grip. The warrior had his club upraised
for another strike. The bayonet slid between his ribs.

Doug jerked the bayonet clear from the convulsed form. The blade was bent and probably could not take another thrust. The remaining warrior was hobbling on his injured foot, trying to get a clear swing with his club. Doug sprang and slashed down the assault rifle. The barrel and bent blade of the bayonet caught the warrior at the juncture of his neck and shoulder. Doug whipped the crumpled butt up to his jaw to finish him.

Next, one of the last two warriors surged back up the mound, club swinging. It swept around level with Doug's knees. Doug sprang above the arc of the club. In midair he kicked out. His foot glanced off the warrior's temple. Doug gripped the rifle lengthwise and slammed it down on the warrior's head as he landed from his leap. The man's body slid back down the pile of rubble.

A stamping kick smashed into Doug's ribs, and he wheeled away to get clear. The final warrior had no weapons except his hands and feet. From the strength of his kick, they might be all he needed. Doug threw the assault rifle in his face, but the warrior batted it aside with a chopping sweep of his arm. In a continuation of the movement, he spun toward Doug in one of the whirling open-hand attacks.

Doug rammed his foot out sideways. It caught the warrior solidly as he spun in. The kick stopped him in midspin. Doug switched legs and snapped up his other foot in an arc. It swiveled the warrior's head. Doug dropped his kicking foot to the ground, then hooked it back up and around. His heel hammered against the warrior's jaw. The warrior fell forward and lay still.

"Well fought, interloper," said an arrogant, familiar voice from behind him.

Doug bent quickly for his discarded war club. He lifted it as he turned.

Cortozca stood atop the mound. He bore the marks of battle, but carried no serious wounds. Apparently he had disdained a firearm for himself. He held his own war club on guard. Doug saw the yellow flame of the Devil Dust madness in his eyes. He realized that the warrior had coldly sacrificed a score of his men to the assault rifle so that he could reach the mound unobserved.

Cortozca laughed. "You almost spoiled my plan, interloper." He hefted his club. "But there is time for us to settle this as warriors should, and then I can still turn the battle my way. I've told you that you would not fare well against me with clubs. I've already proved that once."

Doug thought he heard a high, shrill fluting sound. He ignored it. He remembered vividly the results of his last encounter with the Queen's Warrior when they had contested with clubs. His hands still seemed to feel the ache of his club shattering in his grip beneath Cortozca's blow.

Cortozca might have read his thoughts. He said, "You will not escape me this time, interloper."

Doug shifted grips on his club. "Who said anything about escaping?"

Something strange was happening in the battle below. Ellen saw a tattooed warrior spin around and fall for no apparent reason. Blood shined on his furs. She thought she heard an echoing crack of sound.

"What happened to him?" Tanztra gasped. From where she stood beside Ellen at the narrow temple window, she, too, had seen the man fall. Their view of the battle was limited.

"A sniper!" Ellen cried in sudden realization.

"What?"

Ellen's mind raced as she explained her conjecture. *Could it be . . . ?* She would not let herself finish the thought.

"It may be of no benefit to us," Tanztra said. Then she peered out at the conflict raging below at the main doors to the temple. Ellen looked also. Dalzar's score of warriors were holding their own against a like number of besiegers, few of whom had firearms. War clubs slashed and hewed. Bodies were strewn grotesquely. Ellen shuddered.

They had taken refuge in a large sitting chamber whose narrow windows offered light and a partial view of the action. A stone brazier, suspended from the wall, gave further illumination.

"Listen! What was that?" Tanztra asked.

Ellen heard it too—an unnatural, high-pitched fluting that was strangely familiar. It fluctuated up and down an eerie scale. She could not place its source. She shook her head in annoyance.

"There!" Tanztra's pointing finger drew Ellen's gaze to the uneasy waters of the subterranean sea. Ellen drew in her breath sharply.

Out in the sea, the water churned to froth, and Ellen saw the awful dragon head and serpentine neck rise up from the black waters. Its eyes glowed. And then appeared the broad, pale back of the plesiosaur. The beast shook its head and snapped at the air, as if plagued by some insect. It hissed angrily. Then it extended its neck and churned toward shore with surprising speed. A wide wake rippled out across the water.

Ellen looked at the altar, but there were no sacrifices waiting there, only Mixtek, absorbed in the battle for the temple below him. The High Priest seemed unaware of the monster's appearance.

Up on the stony shore surged the behemoth. Water pooled about its flippered body. It swung its head questingly. Ellen was vaguely aware of the shrill, fluctuating notes that still keened through the cavern. She felt Tanztra grip her arm tightly. The monster lurched toward its familiar altar. It loomed over the structure, fanged jaws opening wide. Too late, Ellen realized its intent. She screamed a warning out the narrow window.

Mixtek might have heard her. Either that or the High Priest somehow sensed the doom upon him. He looked up and around, and froze in terror. Responding to the behavior long ago instilled in it, the God of the Dark Waters sought its customary offering from atop the altar. Mixtek flung up his arms as if in some effort of appeasement. As the fearsome head darted down, Ellen jerked her face away. She heard the High Priest's scream even above the din of battle.

When she looked again, the monster sat uncertainly before the empty altar. Again it snapped at the air and hissed. Ellen realized that the pulsating notes had grown keener. Their resonance bit into her brain. The monster swung away from the altar. Ellen understood with amazement that it was somehow responding to the fluting as it had responded to the ceremonial horn.

Straight toward the temple the plesiosaur shuffled on its flippers. It made surprising speed. A stray warrior sprinted desperately across its path. Its head bobbed down, then up. Ellen had a brief view of kicking legs disappearing down its fanged maw. Her scream mingled with that of Tanztra. The monster shuffled on. They shrank back from the window.

"*El monstruo* is berserk," a sibilant voice hissed at their backs. "I will protect you, *niña,* and you, my Queen."

Ellen wheeled in horror. Aguilar, still in his repellent poncho, stood just within the chamber. She had no idea how he had come to be here. Perhaps he had concealed himself earlier, in hopes of having her at his mercy during the battle.

"You need not fear me, *niña.* I will protect you."

Evil gleamed in his dark eyes. His gaze raked Tanztra. "I will take care of you too, my Queen."

Ellen dug for the .45 in her clothing. Aguilar
crossed the distance between them with the grace of
a leaping cat. His slender hand clamped her wrist
with steely strength. He bent her arm and made her
stagger sidewise. The .45 spun away across the flag-
stones.

Through eyes tearing with pain, Ellen saw Tanztra's silent lunge. Her stone dagger jutted from her
small fist. Aguilar also saw her attack. A thrust of
his arm sent Ellen reeling. He spun away from Tanztra's lunge like a dancer. His grotesque poncho
swirled about his slender figure. One of his seemingly
fragile hands flicked out at Tanztra's extended wrist.
The dagger fell from her fingers. Aguilar struck again
with the heel of his hand. Tanztra's head jerked back
so sharply that her long hair flew straight out. She
wilted limply to the floor.

Ellen ran for the .45. Aguilar's lunging body drove
the breath from her. She grappled frantically with
him, horror surging wild within her. She felt the
knobby bones of his body against her and smelled the
stench of his poncho. His steely hands clamped her
wrists and twisted. Pain shot through her arms and
up to her shoulders. She struggled futilely in his grip.

Behind him, then, Tanztra rose like an avenging
angel. In both hands she gripped the butt of the flaming brazier she had snatched from the wall. While
her hair flew about her face, she swung the brazier

through a full arc like a blazing club. A trail of fire streaked behind it. Aguilar's head was snapped completely around. Fire and coals flew. Tanztra caught him again with the reverse of her swing. His scream was awful. Ellen tore away from him as he toppled, and his head crashed upon the stone floor. The hideous poncho began to burn.

Tanztra dropped the brazier and ran to Ellen, who couldn't take her eyes off Aguilar. She knew with an intuitive certainty that he was dead.

A ghastly scream spun them both. The nightmare head of the plesiosaur rose up past the window. Clasped struggling in its jaws was a screaming warrior. Ellen bit her lip hard. During their fight with Aguilar, the monster had obviously shuffled into the midst of the battling warriors in front of the temple. Ellen realized dimly that the eerie fluting had stopped.

She met Tanztra's frantic, horrified gaze. Would even the temple walls provide protection if the monster turned its wrath upon them? Ellen doubted it. Beyond the heaving bulk of the beast, she could see warriors fleeing. From the sounds, others were trying to fight the creature, god or no. She guessed that it was the warriors loyal to Tanztra, laying down their lives for her.

"Let's get away from the window!" she cried.

They hurried from the chamber. Ellen pulled up short as she saw the figure striding down the passage toward them. "Dick!" she cried.

Tyler halted as he saw them. His condition had worsened since she'd last seen him. There was a peculiar charged intensity behind his features and a hard energy in his movements. The impact of his eyes seemed to rob her of the ability to move.

For a moment he gazed at her. She couldn't read his emotions. He glanced sharply at Tanztra, then seemed to dismiss her. He snapped his eyes back to Ellen. "You're safe now," he said sharply. "Come!"

Ellen hurried to him. "Thank God you're here, Dick. The plesiosaur is outside."

"I know." His eyes shifted out of focus and then back in. "Quickly." He caught her arm. His grip hurt. He all but dragged her down the passage.

She flung a glance back over her shoulder. "Tanztra! Come on!" Surprisingly, the other woman was frowning. But she hesitated only a moment before following them.

Dick hustled her along. He ignored Tanztra. Ellen stole a look at the hard lines of his profile. She saw a stranger. "Dick!" she panted. "Slow down!"

He paid her no heed.

Ellen fought a pang of doubt. Surely there was no need for her to fear Dick.

He appeared to know the temple well, and he halted at a side entrance on the ground level. He still gripped Ellen's arm tightly. Through the doorway she could see only a small segment of the cavern. She could hear screams and yells and gunfire.

Dick's free hand dropped to his waist. For the first

time Ellen noticed his computer and the high-tech walkie-talkie. They were now wired together. The front of the computer's sheath had been cut away to allow access to the keys without removal from the belt. Dick's fingers poised like a dangling spider. Then they danced across the keyboard of the computer. Amplified somehow by the speaker in the walkie-talkie, the high-pitched notes of the computer stabbed through Ellen's skull like tuning forks. She flinched away. His grip held her close. His face carried a terrible intensity. She heard Tanztra's cry.

Turning to the door, Ellen saw the dragon head and long neck writhe sinuously into view from around the corner of the building. The monster shuffled to a halt in front of the door. It bulked huge next to the building. She could see only a part of its enormous mass. An awful odor of moldering dampness and lost ages flared in her nostrils. She turned a horrified, bewildered gaze on Dick.

His glittering eyes met hers exultantly. "You see?" he cried. "The plesiosaur is mine now! *I* control it!" He released her arm. Before she could move, he struck down Tanztra with a single, slashing blow. Then he grabbed Ellen and dragged her from the temple.

Chapter Ten

Doug turned his club to meet Cortozca's first hewing stroke. The impact spun Doug away. The surface of the mound was uneven and littered with bodies. He felt the expended brass cartridges from the AK-47 turn under his feet. Cortozca was upon him before he could set himself. His natural abilities heightened by the drug in his body, the Queen's Warrior moved with bewildering, flashing speed.

Cortozca's club cut down from overhead. Doug got his own weapon up in time. He felt the impact down through the soles of his feet. From overhead, Cortozca cut again. At the last moment, with a massive twitch of his shoulders, he changed the stroke to a horizontal one. Doug shifted his club sideways, held vertical, to intercept the blow. Cortozca's club smashed Doug's own weapon hard against his side, knocking him down the slope of the mound. He wondered if ribs had broken beneath the blow.

Cortozca leaped after him with flames in his eyes.

Doug swung his club to meet the warrior's weapon. The chiseled fangs in the stone mouths clashed together and locked. Doug heaved against Cortozca's club, trying to twist it from his hands. Cortozca's return wrench snapped him from his feet and hurled him aside. He kept his grip on his club and felt it jerk loose from Cortozca's as stone teeth snapped.

They were among the ruins now. Doug glimpsed an outside stairway leading to the flat roof of a one-story building. He could not face the warrior on even terms. These first few strokes had confirmed that. Turning, he ran for the stairs. He felt the wind as Cortozca's club slashed the air in his wake. He sprang up the first three steps, pivoted, and struck in the same motion. His club rebounded from Cortozca's uplifted weapon. The warrior slashed back, flipped over his club deftly, and struck from the other side. Doug retreated up one step before the onslaught, then another. Height did not seem to be giving him an advantage.

Their clubs crashed together. Doug found himself driven steadily upward. He sensed the flat open roof close behind him. Cortozca swung low at his knees. Doug sprang up and back. He felt his heels catch against the uppermost step. He went sprawling backward atop the roof.

He saw Cortozca looming over him like a marble colossus animated by an inner flame of barbaric violence. Cortozca's club slashed down. Doug hooked a foot behind Cortozca's leg and hammered his heel in the back of Cortozca's knee. As Cortozca lurched sideways, Doug kicked hard at his other leg. The stroke of the club hewed off to the side. Cortozca toppled backward and tumbled down the stairs.

Doug came erect with a single movement. He cleared the steps in two descending bounds. Cortozca sprawled at their foot. His club was out of reach. Doug struck down at his prone form. Cortozca shot both hands up to catch the haft of the descending club. The hard stone of the weapon smacked against his palms. He stopped the stroke cold inches above his face.

Up on his feet he surged. Doug shifted grips, and they grappled with the club gripped lengthwise between their chests. Across the club, Cortozca's yellow-eyed face was a leering, demonic visage. Doug felt the awesome strength in the warrior's flexing muscles. Cortozca's sideward yank all but jerked him off his feet. He felt like a rat playing tug-of-war with a terrier. He tried to set his feet for a body throw.

Cortozca snapped his arms out straight and released his grip on the club. Doug went reeling back. But he regained his balance. Cortozca snatched up a section of masonry. Doug doubted that he himself could have lifted it. Cortozca got it overhead with a flawless jerk. The muscles bulged in his arms and chest. He heaved it at Doug.

There was no chance to dodge. Doug swung his club at the missile. The impact went all the way down to his core. The piece of masonry shattered. Doug turned his head away from the rain of fragments.

Cortozca wheeled and caught his own club up from the ground. His bellowing battle cry blasted among the ruins, and it stunned Doug for an instant. Cortozca rushed upon him. Sparks flew as their clubs smashed together and rasped apart. Doug blocked and sidestepped and parried. He was driven back. Pain stretched between his shoulder blades. He realized he was being forced onto the flat roof of a building built at a lower level of the cavern wall.

Cortozca's advance was inexorable. Doug sensed the edge of the roof at his back. Naked stone was twenty feet below. He stood his ground and met Cortozca's attack with his shifting and slashing club.

This could not go on, a detached segment of his mind advised coldly. He was playing Cortozca's game, using Cortozca's choice of weapons. The result, even as Cortozca had warned, seemed inevitable. Cortozca was a master of the war club. But in that mastery, Doug realized suddenly, might lie his only hope.

Cortozca had never trained with other weapons. Just as his static system of unarmed combat rendered him susceptible to other styles, so his narrow expertise with the war club might leave him vulnerable to an unorthodox attack.

Cortozca reared back for a stroke. Doug slid his right hand up to grip his own club's haft just beneath the fanged jaws. Lengthwise, like with a Japanese fighting staff, he thrust it up to meet Cortozca's descending club. The impact flexed his arms down. He stepped in close before Cortozca could strike again. Right and left, he whipsawed his club, snapping first the head and then the butt to Cortozca's jaw. Cortozca shuddered. Doug twirled his club vertical, and smashed the butt straight down on Cortozca's instep, and then rammed the top of it up to his jaw.

Even with strength heightened by the Devil Dust, Cortozca couldn't fully withstand that combination. For the first time in their struggle, he retreated, a single, hobbling step that favored the foot Doug had smashed. He managed to slash with his club as Doug slipped past him into the clear. Cortozca pivoted. He was not even close to finished, Doug realized. But their positions were reversed. It was Cortozca whose back was now to the edge of the roof.

Doug yelled a battle cry of his own. He flung himself forward into a high leaping kick, snapping one foot at Cortozca's chest. Cortozca's club swept up and around to meet his flying form. In midair, Doug parried downward with his club. His foot, with his hurtling weight behind it, crashed full into Cortozca's chest.

Cortozca reeled. His injured foot would not support him. His club slashed impotently at the air as he was driven off the roof. Doug saw him hit the stone below full on his back. He sprawled there. Still gripping his club, Doug sprang from the roof after him. His legs bent deep to absorb the impact of landing.

Stunningly, Cortozca was rising to his feet. The yellow flame still burned in his eyes. He lifted his club. Doug struck first. Shortening his range, he aimed at Cortozca's hands where they gripped the butt of his club. His stroke was accurate. He saw the flame flicker in the demented eyes.

One-handed, Cortozca waved the club at him. His other hand hung useless at his side. Doug skipped clear. He set his feet and swung. The stone fangs of his club bit deep into flesh and bone. Cortozca wavered. Doug gritted his teeth and swung again. The yellow flame in Cortozca's eyes flickered and died. As if the flame had been his soul itself, his body crashed back, lifeless, to the ground.

Doug turned away. It seemed he had been dueling with Cortozca for an eternity. His rifle, he recalled vaguely, was a battered wreck. The strange fluting notes he thought he had heard earlier seemed to puncture his ears. He shook his head. The sounds did not go away. They were not caused by the blows he had taken in combat. He could still hear shouts and cries of battling warriors, but they seemed different somehow. He imagined an edge of panic to them. Frowning, he emerged from the ruins onto the open floor of the cavern. He grimaced at a scent like that of ancient mold.

"So you killed him, Bonner," a voice called from

above. "It only goes to prove that you're more of a savage than he was."

Doug looked up. Fifty feet above, a pair of figures stood locked together on a massive pedestal of stone. Tyler's arm was clamped tightly about Ellen's throat from behind. His other hand manipulated something at his waist. The eerie notes floated in the air. Ellen was terrified.

Doug stared. The notes rose abruptly up the scale. Ellen gave a violent twist of her body and half freed herself from Tyler's stranglehold. "Doug!" she screamed. "Behind you!"

As Doug whirled, he glimpsed a vast, fanged maw plunging down upon him. He saw the enormous scaled bulk of the plesiosaur beyond. The stench of its breath washed over him. Its steam-engine hiss deafened him. He flung himself to the side, landing hard on the rock floor. Inches behind his heel, the fanged jaws snapped shut like a giant steel leghold trap.

He understood dimly that the monster had been waiting for him, almost as if in ambush. Dazed from his fight, his attention drawn by Tyler and Ellen, he had not seen or sensed it behind him. He scrambled to his feet and ran. The cavern spread out before him. There was no cover to be had there, he realized. He felt the rush of displaced air from above and swerved sharply. Beside him, the jaws clashed shut again. He had an instant's impression of the fiery, malignant, and somehow tormented eyes of the beast in its fearsome head.

He swerved again and ran back in close to its bulk. His club was lost somewhere. It would have done him no good, anyway. It would be useless against the monster. He had to reach the cover of the ruins. He saw the enormous flippered bulk lurch toward him as he darted in near. The plesiosaur dipped its head to snap at him again.

He ran clear of its looming bulk. Thwarted, the monster's hissing roar blasted through the cavern. Doug scrabbled up the collapsed remains of an ancient building. Halfway up, he hurled a look back. The monster's gape-jawed head was rushing toward him. He sprang sideways. His feet slipped from under him on the loose debris. He scrabbled upward with clawing fingers. The fluting notes pulsated nightmarishly in his ears.

He reached the summit of the crumbled structure. The monster's head loomed up on a level with him. It seemed baffled by its small, agile prey. Doug jumped as it struck again. He cleared ten feet of open space and came down on a ledge of the cavern wall. Thirty feet away, across open air, Tyler held Ellen helpless while he fingered the keys of what, Doug saw, was his modified computer. He realized fully that Tyler was the master of the beast.

Trapped on the ledge, he spun to face the plesiosaur. Its terrible head swayed hypnotically back and forth before him. He wished he had the AK-47, but even if it was functional, he doubted that it would be effective against the monster. And, absurdly, there still lurked in him a reluctance to do the beast harm. It had never been more than an innocent but deadly puppet in the hands of evil human masters.

The monster drew back its head to strike. Doug braced himself for one last, hopeless, evasive dodge. Subtly the fluting notes changed. Their stridency faded. The monster hesitated. It eyed its cornered prey with baffled and tormented eyes. Doug looked at Tyler. The professor's grin was sadistic and mocking. Clearly he had reined in the beast.

"I've beaten you, Bonner!" he cried. "Admit it! Intellect over savagery. The power of the mind over the strength of the brute!"

"I never wanted you for an enemy!" Doug yelled. He realized for the first time the mad depth of the man's jealous hatred and bitter envy.

"You stole her from me!" Tyler shook Ellen like a doll in front of him. "She was mine until you stole her with your primitive violence!"

Impotently, Doug clenched his fists. He was conscious of the monster's hovering presence, held in check only by the high-tech apparatus at Tyler's waist. The computer was hooked somehow into the walkie-talkie worn beside it. "She was never yours, Tyler!" he shouted. "She never loved you."

"*I* loved *her!*" Tyler shrieked. "I've always loved her! You took her, blast you! You made me look a fool in front of her!"

Doug could see the sick horror in Ellen's face. She appeared helpless in Tyler's maniacal grasp. "Let her go, Tyler!" he cried desperately.

"No! She's mine now! I've won her. I've proven who is the better man! What good are your strength and your fighting abilities now? The rational mind will always triumph over the savagery of the beast. I saw how the plesiosaur reacted to the horn during the ceremony. I realized that the key to controlling it was sound. I interfaced my computer with the audio system of my walkie-talkie, and I went into the cave at night, down into the black depths of it. I called the beast forth, and I trained it! I used my mind and my intellect to control it, just as I've used them to defeat you!" Tyler shoved Ellen aside and down with his last, exultant cry. She lay at his feet, stunned and helpless. Tyler started to laugh. The insane, gobbling sound echoed through the cavern.

Doug looked down at his feet. He knelt as if exhausted and beaten. His hand closed over a round fragment of stone. He gripped it tightly.

"That's right, Bonner, kneel before me! I am your master as surely as I am the master of that poor, brainless creature that holds you helpless."

Doug hefted the stone concealed in his hand. It wasn't so many years since he had pitched baseball in high school. "I'm not your enemy, Tyler!" he yelled.

"The savage is always the foe of the intellectual," Tyler shouted back. "But in the end, it is the intellectual who is always victorious!" The fluting notes rose in shrill triumph.

Doug rose to his feet. He glimpsed the monster beginning its final strike. He threw the stone. Tyler staggered as it smashed full into the walkie-talkie at his waist. Sparks exploded. The computer notes screeched high and shrill. The monster's neck jerked back like a cracking whip. Hissing, it swung its head from side to side as the notes sank into silence. The torment faded from its eyes.

As Tyler screamed in fury, Doug sprang from the ledge. He hit feetfirst against the wall of the cavern and kicked twistingly off to drop the rest of the way to the floor. He ran for the base of the stone pedestal upon which Tyler screamed his rage. He saw the plesiosaur flop backward in confusion.

He found handholds, a quick route up the uneven side of the pedestal. He mounted it with furious precision. As he reached the top, Tyler sprang precariously down the far side. Ellen threw herself into Doug's arms.

"They said you were dead, but I wouldn't believe them!" she gasped. "Dick took me away from Tanztra. He's crazy! I couldn't stop him! When he saw you and Cortozca fighting, he made the monster wait."

"It's over," Doug told her. "But I've still got to go after him. We can't leave him loose. He's a danger to himself and everyone else."

"I'm going with you."

Doug didn't argue. He didn't want to leave her alone again.

Tyler had reach the cavern floor and was sprinting away. Freed of its auditory bonds, the monster was wandering about the cavern. It snapped in irritation at fleeing warriors. Doug hoped it would go back to the lake.

When they reached the ground, Doug caught Ellen's hand and they ran after Tyler. Seeing where the professor was headed, he released Ellen's hand and sprinted ahead. It was no good. Tyler's lead was too great. Just once, Tyler stopped and flung a glance at his pursuers. Doug was closing in fast. Tyler's face was wild. He turned and plunged into the Chamber of Whispering Death.

Doug pulled up short. Ellen reached him, panting, a moment later. They stared into the darkness.

"He doesn't have a light," Ellen whispered. There were no sounds from within the chamber.

They turned as a familiar figure ran up to them. Warmly, Doug gripped hands with Dalzar. "Men of both sides saw you kill Cortozca," the warrior said in awe.

"Mixtek is dead too," Ellen told him with a shudder. "The monster got him. And Tanztra killed Aguilar."

"Mixtek's warriors are surrendering," Dalzar said. "We've won." He looked from them into the chamber. "I saw your companion flee in there."

"He's gone mad," Doug said. "Send men out into

the valley to intercept him if he makes it through the chamber. Don't hurt him."

Dalzar nodded and started to turn away. A cracking came from within the cave. It became a roar. Somewhere in those black depths, Tyler must have stepped wrong. Stone crashed down on stone in the darkness.

An awful cry came from the cave. It was a shriek of anger and denial, of bitterness and hatred. The sound flung itself back and forth inside the Chamber of Whispering Death. Ellen buried her face against Doug's shoulder. A louder crash resounded from the cave, and then another. Doug backed away, drawing Ellen with him.

Each crash of stone seemed to generate another. The reverberations were feeding off themselves. Doug had a horrible image of Tyler trapped and crushed in the awful darkness with the bones of the dead. A detonation of sound, louder than anything before, rolled out of the tunnel. Doug saw a crack split the wall above the chamber's mouth. Like a jagged bolt of black lightning, it zigzagged up the wall of the great cavern, then spread like a spiderweb across the ceiling far overhead. Dust and pebbles rained down on them. The ground gave a horrible, familiar tremor beneath Doug's feet. It was stronger than any of the others he had felt.

"Earthquake!" he shouted. Somehow, the cataclysmic collapse of the ceiling in the chamber had triggered an upheaval in the unstable strata beneath them. "Let's get out of here! This whole place could come down!"

"Tanztra!" Ellen's cry stopped him. "She's in the temple—unconscious, I think!"

"I'll get her!" Doug cried. "Go on with Dalzar." She hesitated, staring at him. "Go!" he shouted. "I'll be faster alone."

She read the truth of his words. "The side entrance!" she said. She ran with Dalzar toward the mouth of the cavern. Warriors were also racing toward the exit. Overhead, the crack widened and spread across the ceiling with great blasts of sound.

Doug ran for the temple while the floor vibrated beneath his pounding feet. Larger and larger fragments of stone crashed down. He saw the ruins of the city shivering and collapsing into rubble.

He staggered through the side entrance to the temple. Tanztra was there, sprawled on the floor and moving feebly. He lifted her in his arms. As he ducked out through the doorway, the temple imploded and the walls toppled inward, the roof collapsing upon it. An enormous crack opened in front of the altar where the plesiosaur had been offered its victims. Then the entire altar tipped forward and disappeared into the pit.

Tanztra was clasped in his arms. He ran. The ground heaved up and flung him from his feet. He tried to cushion Tanztra's fall. He gathered her up again and made it upright. Her hair brushed like a ghost against his arms. He stumbled into a running stride once more.

His legs began to want to take their own directions. Ahead of him, the floor split open. The crack widened and seemed to rush to meet him. On its edge, he sprang far out with Tanztra in his arms. Blackness flashed beneath him. He came down hard. He felt himself tilt backward, and threw his weight forward. Tottering, he ran on.

The arched mouth of the cavern was in front of him. Stones plummeted from above. He drew a last burst of speed from his faltering legs. A fragment of ceiling, large enough to have crushed the plesiosaur, smashed to pieces only yards behind him. The thunder of its fall rang throughout the cavern.

Then Dalzar was there, reaching to take the Queen from his arms. The warrior raced on ahead. Doug looked back. Debris rained down into the lake. He saw the plesiosaur slither into the dark water. Broad horizontal sweeps of its tail sent it down toward the safety of the depths. Doug ran out onto the valley floor into the waiting ranks of people.

He turned just in time to see the whole huge overhang collapse in front of the cavern mouth and bury it completely.

"I hope it wasn't killed during the earthquake." Ellen's voice was almost wistful. "I like to think of it living in the lake without being bothered by anyone."

Doug remembered his own reluctance to see harm come to the plesiosaur. He followed Ellen's gaze to the great pile of stone and rubble that was all that remained of the enormous cavern mouth. The earthquake had sealed the ruins and the plesiosaur and the Fire Lichen from the sight of man. Doug squeezed Ellen's hand. "I think he made it. I saw him go into the water, and the lake's deep enough to protect him. He's probably glad to be rid of us pesky humans."

Ellen smiled gratefully up at him and returned the pressure of his hand. Together they strolled through the village from Tanztra's home and then turned back. People were resuming normal life after the earthquake and power struggle of the day before. With the deaths of Mixtek and Cortozca, the revolt had collapsed, and Tanztra had accepted renewed oaths of allegiance from the rebel warrior who had survived the battle.

"Poor Dick." Ellen shook her head. "I wish I could have talked to him. But he never gave me the chance. I never knew how he felt."

"It's not your fault," Doug assured her. Tyler's body had not been recovered. The outer exit to the Chamber of Whispering Death had also been sealed by the earthquake. It had become the tomb of yet another warrior. "You can't blame yourself."

She nodded. "I know." An undertone of resiliency was in her voice. Her eyes brightened. "Look." She pointed to the balcony of the Queen's house.

The Queen stood very close to Dalzar's tall form.

She was gazing intently up at him as he spoke to her. He gestured out across the village. "Dalzar will make a good Queen's Warrior," Doug said. He glanced at Ellen. "I suppose you want to take matchmaker's credit for bringing them together?"

"They just needed a little help."

"That's not all they'll need help with."

Ellen caught his meaning immediately. "I know. It won't be easy for them or Quaztar, will it?"

Doug nodded. His body was bruised and sore, but he had suffered no permanent injury from his trials. He gazed at the stone village. Already, bandits and drug dealers had found their way here to intrude on the ancient isolation of this remnant of a lost civilization. How much longer would it be before other predators invaded Quaztar?

"They need some contact with the outside." Ellen seemed to have read his thoughts. "The children are all sickly. Medical treatment would restore their health."

The blessings of civilization versus the curses of it, Doug thought. Could Tanztra and Dalzar, for all their innate wisdom and intelligence, balance one against the other? Or would the basic simplicity of their race be overwhelmed by the influx of high-tech, modern mankind?

"You like it here, don't you?" Ellen asked him softly.

Doug nodded. "Maybe Tyler was right," he said thoughtfully. "Maybe I'm a warrior at heart." He looked down into her eyes. "We could stay and help them," he suggested cautiously.

Ellen blinked. Her eyes seemed to grow brighter. "What do you mean?"

Doug thought the idea through. "My job for the DEA is done. Aguilar is dead and the source of the Devil Dust is gone. Besides, I'm feeling too old for this kind of work. I've got contacts in the State Department. I could probably get a position with them as an on-the-spot consultant on Quaztar, an independent kingdom inside Peru."

"And the university would probably give me a grant to do field research!" Ellen added breathlessly. "We could live here for as long as it takes to help Tanztra deal with the outside world. I even tried to tell Dick that I was more comfortable here with Tanztra than in most so-called civilized places."

Doug looked away from her shining face. He gazed up at the ceiling of mist overhead. With a growing satisfaction, he knew that what he'd been planning to say was right.

"There's one other thing." He looked back at Ellen as he spoke.

"What's that?"

"It's on a personal note. About us. Do you approve of living together?"

"Doug!" she exclaimed.

He nodded. "Good. Neither do I. We'll have to get married." He took her hand. "Will you marry me, Ellen? I love you."

"Yes!" She came eagerly into his embrace. "I love you too."

Doug held her. People were watching them. It didn't matter. Soon, they would all be neighbors. The sense of satisfaction grew within him. There would be problems and struggles for them and for Quaztar in the future. But that was all right too. A warrior must always expect another battle. Luckily, he would have Ellen to come home to.